Clara's Gree<u> </u>

CW00518177

For Stephen Nelson.
Yes, Dad, I've just outed your middle name to the entire world.
I love you.

Chapter 1

Twirling around in front of the mirror, I smile at my reflection as I admire my sparkly new purchase. The intricate beading on the kaftan dazzles beneath the bright lights, making me believe I'm only seconds away from the beach. Taking a step back, my stomach flutters with excitement as I slip my feet into a pair of strappy sandals and rest my hand on my hip. The glitzy girl in the mirror beams back at me, as though she's a different person entirely to the woman standing in front of it.

I run my fingers over the delicate fabric and allow my eyes to close, imagining salty sea air blowing through my hair. Almost instantly, I am transported to a stunning turquoise ocean. I can almost feel the soft sand between my toes as I inhale deeply and lose myself in the daydream. Pelicans soar in the distance as I gently sway back and forth in the world's comfiest hammock, totally oblivious to anything other than the blissful sound of the waves lapping against the shore...

'That makes your arse look big...'

Spinning around, I scowl at the laptop and look down at my outfit sceptically. 'It does?'

'I'm joking!' Lianna chuckles, leaning towards her webcam and bursting into laughter. 'It's fabulous, but I don't think you really need another kaftan. We're only going for five days. How much can you possibly wear in such a short space of time?'

A quick second glance in the mirror is all it takes to convince myself that I *do* need another kaftan. I can nearly hear my reflection egging me on as I give my overflowing suitcase a dubious look and wonder how much more I can realistically fit inside without bursting the clasp.

'It's coming with me.' Not hesitating for a moment longer, I whip the embellished garment over my head and throw open the case.

'How can you *still* have room in there?' Lianna exclaims, taking a sip of wine and propping her phone up on her knees. 'That suitcase is like Mary Poppins' handbag!'

Ignoring her comments, I fold the kaftan and desperately try to make some room amongst the assortment of brightly coloured clothes. Resorting to squashing down my many pairs of shoes, I sit on the case and bounce up and down in an attempt to flatten the contents. Numerous groans escape my lips as I furiously wrestle with my beach bag to create some much-needed space. The mattress squeaks beneath me, providing a comical soundtrack to the rather unflattering scene. Not ready to give up, I take a running jump and land on the case with a thud.

'You have no idea how ridiculous you look right now.' Holding her phone an inch from her face, Li giggles and takes a screenshot. 'This will make great blackmail material for the next time I want to borrow your Versace stilettos.'

'You better delete that picture. No one needs to see me humping a suitcase in my underwear.' Huffing and puffing as I fight with the flimsy lock, I catch a glimpse of myself in the mirror and frown. 'Besides, you're *never* borrowing my shoes again because you stretch them out with your big clown feet.'

Hearing her click away regardless, I continue with my mission until the lock finally surrenders and allows the case to close.

'Finally!' Lianna cheers, clapping her hands together as I fist pump the air in victory. 'Can I show you *my* holiday outfits now?'

Taking a moment to catch my breath, I throw myself on the bed and adjust my bra to avoid an embarrassing wardrobe malfunction. 'Shoot...'

'I think we'll start with my swimwear.' She says to the camera, tipping out the contents of numerous plastic bags onto her bedroom floor. 'I mean, it's going to be boiling in Greece. I don't think we will be wearing much else...'

As Li drags her pink suitcase into view, I pull my laptop towards me and allow my mind to wander. We leave for Mykonos in less than twenty-four hours, but only now have we slowed down enough to be able to pack. To say that our working lives have been busy lately would be a massive understatement. Not that I'm complaining, I still remember the days when I prayed for the business to be as thriving as it is right now. Although it doesn't feel like it, a full twelve months have drifted by since Suave secured the Ianthe collaboration and in that time the company has gone from strength to strength.

When we first discovered that Janie had coerced Stelios Christopoulos into signing the all-important contract, we didn't have much time to envisage the public's reaction to the partnership. With Suave being so close to the brink of destruction at the time, all efforts were thrown into bringing the collaboration to life as quickly as possible and it paid off in more ways than we could have ever imagined.

The limited-edition pieces, tastefully labelled *The Rhodantha Collection*, literally flew off the shelves. Within a matter of days, the entire collection sold out completely, leaving Ianthe with a big decision to make. They could either sign another contract or pocket the profits and move on to new ventures. Taking into consideration the huge popularity of the partnership, Stelios didn't think twice about signing an agreement that would see the two companies work together for the foreseeable future and the results have been *amazing*.

Since then, the Suave office has been a fabulous place to be. No longer do we lie awake at night worrying about how to pay people's wages. No longer do we frantically call around other companies in a desperate bid for business and no longer are we at loggerheads with one another over how to turn things around. I'm pleased to say the only thing keeping me awake at night is the dilemma over which savings account I should use for Noah. Come nightfall, I have so many figures whirring around my mind and each one makes my stomach flutter with adrenaline.

The truth is, Oliver and I have never been in financial difficulty, but the huge success of the Ianthe deal has left us with more money than we know what to do with. This vast turnaround of events has been a lot to take in and not just for me, but for all of my friends, too. With the cheques rolling in and the figures on our bank statements growing rapidly, it's easy to forget that just a year ago things were very different indeed and I'm always secretly concerned we could end up back there.

My conservative nature has meant the majority of our money is tied up in high-interest accounts, but I can't say the same for Lianna and Vernon. Those two flash the cash like there's no tomorrow, as do Marc and Gina. Being a director in a company that turns over millions of pounds certainly comes with its fair share of perks, but as strange as this may sound, it takes a lot of getting used to. Seeing my friends purchase luxury cars and expensive jewellery is bizarrely surreal and as much as I try to join in, my inner saveaholic stops me from doing so.

I'd like to say Janie is equally as cautious with her new-found wealth, but the reality is she spends Stelios's money like it's going out of fashion. Living the high life in Mykonos, my crazy mother-in-law has taken to her dramatic lifestyle change like Carrie Bradshaw to a Manolo Blahnik sale. I still find it hard to believe that while we're going about our day-to-day lives, Janie is sitting on her throne in Stelios's beachside mansion like a Greek goddess. Well, if Greek goddesses drank whiskey, swore like sailors and wore extremely inappropriate clothing, but still, you get the picture.

Oliver is yet to accept his mother's relationship with Stelios and I'm beginning to think he never will. Regardless of Janie being happier than I have ever seen her, Oliver just cannot see beyond Stelios's past. His infamous sex tape with Giulia Romano is something we no longer speak about, but I know it is all Oliver can see when I dare to breathe Stelios's name. Oliver still won't have custard on his desserts and I can't say I blame him. That notorious video is the reason I skip custard creams with my morning coffee, but I am quietly grateful. The absence of my beloved breakfast biscuits has resulted in the loss of my muffin top and that's *always* a good thing.

In spite of Oliver's feelings towards Stelios, I'm hoping beyond hope this trip will change his mind about Janie's choice of partner. Receiving pictures and Facebook updates only give Oliver a snapshot of his mother's life. It doesn't allow him to see that beneath the photographs and online displays of affection, is a relationship that is proving all the doubters wrong. As hard as it is to believe, Janie and Stelios appear to be deeply in love. To be fair, their love does centre around a fondness for ouzo, tacky furniture and a frankly horrific dress sense, but I suppose love is love, no matter where it is found.

I am praying that once Oliver immerses himself in his mother's new life, he will see just how good for her Stelios Christopoulos really is. For reasons I am yet to understand, Stelios seems to love Janie just the way she is. His ability to see past her potty mouth and impudent behaviour is bringing out a whole new side to the Janie we know and love. If Instagram posts are to be believed, Stelios is certain he's finally found *The One,* but after three failed marriages and numerous high-profile relationships with notorious celebrities, I'm not holding my breath.

'What do you think of this bikini?' Lianna asks suddenly, popping my thought bubble and bringing me back to the task at hand. 'Is it too much?'

Snapping to attention, I blink at the screen and raise my eyebrows. The rope-style swimsuit wraps around her toned body numerous times, barely covering her modesty with a series of thoughtfully placed ribbons.

'It will make for some rather interesting tan lines, that's for sure.' I mumble, rolling onto my stomach and yawning loudly. 'Can you really call it a bikini when it's made of a single piece of string?'

Shrugging her shoulders, Li dances around in front of the webcam. 'What you are referring to as *a piece of string* is actually haute couture...'

Tearing off the label, she throws on a crochet sarong before diving back into the pile of clothes on the floor.

'Do you really think that's suitable swimwear for this trip?' I ask, already knowing that it most certainly is not. 'What's wrong with a classic swimming costume?'

Quickly tugging on a pair of denim shorts, she grabs her sunglasses and ruffles her blonde hair. 'Clara, we're going to visit Janie. *Anything* is suitable for this holiday.'

Not being able to argue with her, I nod along and crawl under the duvet. 'That's true, but it's not exactly a holiday, is it? Don't forget why we're going to Mykonos in the first place...'

When Stelios invited Suave's board of directors to his annual Ice Party, I didn't think Oliver and I would be in attendance. After all, with Oliver's detest of Stelios growing stronger by the day, I couldn't envisage us clinking glasses under a Greek sun and toasting new ventures anytime soon. Nevertheless, when business calls, Oliver has no choice but to put his personal opinions to one side and represent our company.

You see, Stelios's yearly gathering for his business associates is a very exclusive event and this year, Suave was lucky enough to receive an invite. The famous Ice Party is held at Stelios's Mykonos mansion and is attended by all his trade contacts. This luxury event gives his colleagues a chance to network and make new connections within the industry. Or at least, that's what he tells his bank manager. The reality is that Stelios's legendary parties are just a chance for him to spend more of his money before the taxman gets his grubby hands on it. Although, he must have one hell of an accountant to get away with putting scantily clad dancers and caviar canapés through as a tax write-off.

'I'm telling you, Clara. This is going to be the holiday of a lifetime.' Lianna sings, returning into view wearing a cute white dress. 'No children, loads of cash and the old gang back together again. It's going to be unforgettable!'

I smile back at my best friend as a wave of adrenaline washes over me. With Owen and Eve staying behind with the twins, Hugh running the business and Dawn in control of Floral Fizz, it is down to Oliver, Li, Vernon, Marc and I to wave the flag for Suave. Of course, when Gina found out about this trip she immediately arranged childcare for Madison, MJ and Melrose and booked herself a plane ticket. In her words, there was absolutely no way Marc was escaping parental duties to tan his arse in Greece and leaving her behind.

I do feel a little guilty to be jetting off without Noah, but the thought of a Greek adventure with my friends makes me all warm and giddy inside. I can't remember the last time we spent some proper time together outside of the office and I definitely can't remember the last time Oliver and I did *anything* without having Noah between us.

When you have a playful six-year-old keeping you busy, it's easy to neglect your time as husband and wife. Slowly but surely, romantic date nights are replaced with rainy visits to the zoo and mammoth Lego sessions. This trip to Mykonos is exactly what the doctor ordered to relight the fire in our relationship. Lazy days on the beach and candlelit dinners beneath the moonlight await. I can almost taste the pína coladas...

'How's Oliver feeling about this holiday now?' Lianna asks, holding up two pairs of high-heeled wedges. 'Is he looking forward to it yet?'

Pointing at the pink pair of shoes, I shake my head in response as the reality of Oliver's attitude towards this trip comes back to haunt me. 'He's still refusing to acknowledge this as anything more than a networking opportunity. Although, I did catch him dancing around to Club Tropicana while he packed his sunscreen earlier.'

Lianna laughs and tosses the pink wedges into her suitcase carelessly. 'He'll come around to Stelios eventually. He has to. Stelios has been in our lives for an entire year now. His collaboration with Suave and relationship with Janie are both going strong. You've got to hand it to him, Stelios must be doing something right.'

I nod along as she speaks, hoping that she's right. 'I think a lot of Oliver's hostility towards Stelios comes from his anxiety over his mother. He would never admit it, but you know how much he worries about Janie. The fact that we haven't seen her for a year has just added fuel to the fire.'

'She didn't plan this move very well, did she?' Li muses, looking around her messy bedroom. 'Who goes on holiday and never comes back? If she was *my* mother, I'd be worried, too.'

'Exactly!' I reply, grabbing a pillow and curling up into a tiny ball. 'Let's face it, the idea of Janie being thousands of miles away without supervision is nerve-racking for all of us.'

Continuing to throw various items into her suitcase, Li shoots me a wink. 'Clara, she's living in a Greek mansion with an eccentric billionaire for company. Just how much trouble could she possibly get into?'

I close my eyes and picture my audacious mother-in-law sprawled out in a luxury residence, with immediate access to millions of pounds at her fingertips.

'You know what, Li? I dread to think...'

Chapter 2

Splashes of water land on my face as I float on my back in the warm ocean, providing welcome relief from the sweltering heat. Tipping back my head, I smile as rays of sunshine bounce off the waves, creating a sparkling display all around me. Gently kicking my legs, I screw up my nose as the droplets become heavier and heavier, until I am practically drowning beneath their weight...

'Clara?' A tinny voice echoes in the distance. 'Clara?'

Letting out a sleepy moan, I rub my face as I stir in my slumber.

'*Clara!*'

Struggling to pinpoint the voice, I peel open my eyes and bat away an excited Pumpkin, who is happily licking my face in a bid to wake me from my deep sleep.

'What time is it?' I murmur, unable to hide my disappointment at discovering I am still sprawled out on the bed and *not* floating in the ocean in Mykonos.

'It's dinner time.' Oliver says lightly, looking around the untidy bedroom and frowning. 'Please tell me you've packed and why are you in your underwear?'

Yawning groggily, I push myself into a sitting position. 'I was trying on holiday clothes earlier and I must have fallen asleep. I have packed though. Well, almost...'

Oliver motions to the messy bedroom once more and scowls. 'Did a tornado hit while you were doing it?'

I giggle at his appalled expression and pull the sheets up to my chin. 'Don't worry! I'll clear it all away.'

Reaching up, I pull him down onto the bed and wrap my arms around his waist. His dark curls flop into his face as I nuzzle my nose into his warm neck. Resisting the urge to fall back into a delicious sleep, I force my eyes open and clear my throat.

'So, less than twenty-four hours to go!' I say happily, my eyes glinting with anticipation. 'Are you excited yet?'

Oliver shakes his head dismissively, but I notice a slight smile in his eyes before he corrects it with a scowl. 'To be completely honest, I'd rather stay behind with Noah. It sure doesn't take five of us to represent the company.'

'Oh, don't be such a spoilsport.' Resting my chin on his chest, I look up at him and grin widely. 'Just think of the sunshine...'

'The sun shines fine here.' He retorts quickly, not missing a beat.

'In London?' I reply with a scoff. 'We haven't seen the sun for months!'

Choosing to ignore me, Oliver closes his eyes.

'The beaches in Mykonos are said to be incredible...' I whisper, trying to win him over with his love of the beach.

'We have beaches here, too.' Defiantly sticking out his chin, Oliver strokes Pumpkin's head as she curls up next to him. 'We don't need to jump on a plane to go to the damn beach.'

Biting my lip, I rack my brains for something he can't argue with. 'You will get to see your mum. That's pretty exciting.'

'I guess...' Reluctantly nodding, he rhythmically runs his fingers along my spine. 'I'm starting to forget what she looks like.'

There's a short silence, which I worry Oliver will fill with a rant about Stelios and I try to move the conversation along.

'Plus, we have five whole days on a beautiful Greek island to enjoy.' Inhaling deeply, I drag my bare legs over the sheets and sigh. 'How long has it been since we had a holiday?'

Drumming his fingers on my back, Oliver looks up at the ceiling. 'We went to Chester when my dad and Courtney visited a few months back.'

'City breaks don't count! When did we last have a *proper* holiday?' I ask, rolling onto my back. 'When did you last feel hot sun on your skin? When did you last feel sand between your toes, or swim in an ocean that's as deep as forever?'

Oliver appears deep in thought and pulls me towards him as I speak.

'It's been years since we last left the country.' I persist, casting my mind back to our visit to Florida. 'Travel is good for the soul. Leaving yourself behind and forgetting your responsibilities, even just for a short while, brings you back to life.'

Planting a kiss on my forehead, Oliver squeezes me tightly and laughs. 'You make it sound so romantic.'

'It *is* romantic!' I cry, glad that he's finally showing a tiny bit of enthusiasm. 'Sun, sea and sand await...'

A loud bang from the living room snaps us out of our bubble and Oliver takes it as his cue to leave.

'Until then, you have a dog that needs feeding, a child who needs bathing and a husband who wants the bedroom clearing of your sh... *belongings*.'

Giving him a salute as he tosses me a dressing gown and disappears into the living room, I enjoy the tingle of adrenaline in my stomach. That magical holiday feeling is slowly taking over my ability to function like I usually do and as such, my daily tasks are requiring extra effort.

Allowing myself a final stretch before jumping to my feet, I slip on the dressing gown and jump over a pile of discarded bikinis on the carpet.

'Alright!' I say brightly, following in Oliver's footsteps and striding into the living room. 'What would everyone like for dinner?'

'Pizza!' Noah yells, looking up from his football sticker book and grinning. 'The answer is always pizza!'

Knowing that once he goes to my mother's tomorrow he will be force-fed her homemade health-driven meals until we collect him after our trip, I peek at Oliver and smile when he nods in agreement.

'Pizza it is.' I flash Noah the thumbs-up sign as Oliver grabs his car keys.

'I'll go get it.' Oliver sighs, ushering Pumpkin onto the balcony. 'By the time I get back, I want that damn bedroom clean!' With a friendly wink, he tugs on his jacket and walks out of the apartment, leaving Noah and I alone on the couch.

'When *I* don't tidy my room, I have to give up one of my toys for a day.' Noah says, smiling mischievously. 'Are you going to have one of *your* toys confiscated?'

Tickling him under the chin, I take a sticker of a Manchester United player and place it in the corresponding space. 'Are you looking forward to going to Grandma's tomorrow?'

Nodding enthusiastically, Noah brushes his curly hair out of his face. 'Grandad is taking me to watch football and Grandma is taking me fossil hunting.'

'Fossil hunting?' I repeat, pointing to another sticker as he scours the page for the correct space.

'We're going to climb the mountain and crack open the rocks to find dinosaurs.' He says seriously, keeping his eyes fixed on the sticker book as he speaks.

'Wow!' Knowing that fossil hunting is probably the least weird and wonderful activity my wacky mother will have planned for him, I breeze straight past it. 'Are you going to miss us while we're away?'

Considering my question for a moment, Noah shakes his head firmly. 'No.'

'No?' I gasp in mock horror. 'Why?'

'It's only five days.' He replies, reaching up and kissing my cheek. 'Don't be sad.'

'I'm not sad.' Resting my chin on his head, I shuffle closer to him. 'I'm just going to miss you a little bit, that's all.'

'You're going on holiday with Dad and I'm going on holiday with Pumpkin.' He looks up at me and blinks his big eyes repeatedly. 'We're all going to have fun.'

Smiling down at him, I wonder when my baby boy became so grown up. 'You're such a clever boy, Noah.'

'Of course, I am.' He replies confidently. 'I'm six.'

Giggling at his response, I hug him closely as Pumpkin tears back into the apartment and dives onto the sofa next to us.

'Are *you* looking forward to going to Grandma's house?' I whisper to Pumpkin, who has rested her fluffy snout on my lap. A happy wag of her tail confirms to me that she is. 'Maybe *you* will be lucky enough to go fossil hunting, too.'

'Pumpkin *has* to come.' With a serious expression on his face, Noah pats Pumpkin's head. 'She has to protect us from the dinosaurs.'

'Did you hear that, Pumpkin? You've got an important job to do.' Sliding off the couch, I wander over to the computer desk and sit down in the leather office chair. 'Perhaps you will need a security guard uniform...'

'Grandma's already got her one.' Noah says proudly. 'It has a badge on the front and a real torch.'

Not doubting him for a second, I decide not to question it. Noah could tell me my mum is teaching Pumpkin how to read tarot cards and I'd still believe him.

Leaving him to his football stickers, I wiggle the mouse to bring the computer monitor to life and spin around in the chair. Almost immediately, our plane tickets flash up on the screen and I feel my lips stretch into a smile. Quickly running my eyes over the details, I click *print* and sit back as the printer springs into action. The steady sound of the machine is quietly mesmerising as I watch the tickets magically appear on the paper in front of me.

It's hard to believe this time tomorrow we shall be in Greece and it's even harder to believe we're going to be child-free. This shall be my first visit to Mykonos and to be discovering the island from Stelios's lavish mansion is just the icing on the cake. For weeks I've been fawning over images of whitewashed buildings and iconic blue doors online, just wishing to dive into the screen and lose myself in the beautiful pictures.

Tearing myself away from the computer, I walk into the bathroom and set the taps running on the bathtub. Hot water splashes into the bath, causing a babbling pool to form in the bottom of the tub. Scouring the cabinet, I select one of my favourite bath bombs and drop it into the water. The pretty sphere melts into the bubbles, creating a beautiful rainbow of colour as the tub rapidly fills with frothy suds.

Leaning against the sink, I listen to the sound of running water and check out my reflection in the mirror. My blue peepers are carrying some rather large bags and my pale skin is crying out for a hefty dose of sunshine. These days, I don't really pay much attention to my appearance. Unless Oliver and I are going on a rare date or meeting friends for a quick cocktail, I only look in the mirror to apply a quick slick of mascara and a dab of lipstick. Finding the time every morning to paint my face on is near impossible. Cooking breakfast, walking Pumpkin and responding to emails take priority over contouring my tired face into oblivion. I'm starting to realise being a mother, a wife, a company director and a dog owner does that to you.

Reminding myself I shall soon be on a plane out of here, I smile cheerily and pop my head back into the living room.

'Noah, it's time for your bath.'

'Can't I have my bath after dinner?' He asks, already knowing the answer is going to be *no*. 'I want my pizza first.'

Pretending to chew over his request for a few seconds, I inhale sharply before speaking. 'I'm afraid not. Bath, pizza and then early to bed.'

'But it's the school holidays!' Putting down his sticker book, he slides off the couch and groans. 'Why do I have to go to bed early tonight?'

'Because Grandma will be here to pick you up very early tomorrow and I want you to have a good night's sleep.' Ushering him into the bathroom, I check the water temperature before turning off the taps. 'The sooner you get in there, the sooner you will be eating pizza.'

With a final smile, I fold a towel and leave it next to the tub before slipping out of the bathroom.

'I'm going to finish my packing.' I yell over my shoulder, as Pumpkin follows me across the living room. 'If you need me, just shout.'

'Mum...' Noah's voice travels after me as I pluck a pile of fresh laundry from the armchair.

Trying to juggle the stack of clothes, I walk back to the bathroom and push open the door. 'Yes?'

'Don't forget to pack a sun hat.' Placing a blob of bubbles onto his nose, he blows them into the air and laughs as they fall around him like snow. 'You don't want to get sunstroke.'

I smile back at him, wondering where he gets his random snippets of wisdom. 'When did you become so smart?'

'When I started school.' He replies, squirting shampoo into his hands and lathering up. 'School makes everyone smart.'

Proudly watching him wash his hair, I silently remark at how much Noah has grown up over the past twelve months. I must admit we did have some teething problems with his behaviour before he started school, but since his sixth birthday we really seem to have turned a corner. He's finally settled into his own personality and becoming a fine young man in the process. His manners are impeccable, he always wears a smile and he looks more like Oliver than Oliver himself.

'Pizza will be here soon.' Noah warns, shaking the excess water out of his hair. 'You better hurry if you want to finish your packing before Dad gets home.'

Playfully splashing water at me, he giggles as I hide for cover behind the laundry.

'You're the boss, Noah. You're the boss...'

Chapter 3

'And here are his pyjamas and an extra coat...'
Hurriedly handing over yet more bags to my mother, I
give her a strained smile and nervously squeeze my
hands into tight fists. 'Oh, and you should take his
scarf, because you never know with the weather here,
do you?'

'Clara, just relax!' My mum laughs and shakes her
head gently. 'It's the height of summer!'

Not feeling reassured, I read over my checklist for
what feels like the hundredth time in search of
anything I might have missed.

'Do you have a lead for Pumpkin?' I ask, heading
into the kitchen to retrieve one.

'Yes.' She replies quickly, whistling for Pumpkin to
join her and Noah by the door. 'We've also bought her
a harness and some new bowls. Pink, to match her
collar.'

Smiling thinly, I try to ignore the growing nausea in
my stomach. 'What about Noah's toothbrush? I don't
recall packing one...'

'I saw you put it in here earlier.' Tapping one of the
bags, she purses her lips and exhales loudly. 'You're
becoming hysterical, Clara. I can always pick up
anything you have missed. You're only going for five
days.'

Not taking my eyes off my checklist, I tap my foot
impatiently and frown.

'Well, I think that's everything.' She says
confidently, ruffling Noah's hair as she picks up the

collection of bags at her feet. 'Are you ready to go, Noah?'

'Do you have to go right now?' I stammer, before he can reply. 'Why don't we have a coffee first? Or a quick bite to eat?'

'Noah, give your mom a hug.' Oliver instructs, dragging our suitcases into the living room and placing them next to the couch. 'I think she needs one.'

I feel my cheeks flush as Noah tugs on his backpack and wraps his arms around my waist.

'Don't worry, Mummy.' He says softly. 'Pumpkin and I are going to be just fine.'

'Make sure you're a good boy for Grandma and Grandad, okay?' Holding him closely, I kiss his chubby cheeks and force myself to smile. 'I'll bring you back a lovely present.'

Noah's eyes light up at the mention of a gift and he claps his hands together. 'Can I have a unicorn? Oh, please can I have a unicorn?'

'Erm...' I laugh lightly and look up at Oliver. 'I'm not sure there are any unicorns in Greece, Noah.'

'Or a seahorse?' He asks excitedly, a huge grin on his face as he jumps up and down on the spot. 'If you can't find a unicorn, may I have a seahorse?'

'I'll... I'll try my best.' Giving him a final cuddle, I usher him towards my mum as she pushes open the door. 'Go on. Grandad will be waiting for you.'

'Have a good time, buddy.' Oliver says, giving Noah a high-five as he takes Pumpkin by the lead. 'Enjoy the fossil hunting and make sure you cheer on the reds at the football...'

As Oliver says his goodbyes to Noah, my mum holds out her arms for a hug.

'Have a great trip!' She whispers into my ear. 'Don't worry about Noah and Pumpkin. They'll be having more fun than you guys.'

Nodding in response, I smile as Pumpkin licks my hand and stares intently at her lead, itching to get going.

'Alright!' My mother trills, leading the way out into the lobby. 'Let's go!'

'Bye!' Waving as they disappear into the lift, I feel a lump form in my throat and try to shake it off.

'Am I pathetic for not wanting to leave him for a few days?' I ask Oliver, my voice starting to crack with emotion.

'I don't know.' He replies with a sigh, wrapping his arms around my shoulders. 'We've never left him before, so I'm not sure how we're supposed to feel. Why don't you phone Gina and ask...'

'*Whoop! Whoop!*' A familiar voice yells, causing Oliver and I to exchange confused glances. 'Let's get this party started!'

Stepping into view, Gina leaves Marc to carry their cases down the staircase and dances along the lobby. 'We're free! We're free of kids for five whole days! Quick! Somebody pinch me!'

Oliver laughs and kisses my forehead. 'I think that answers your question, Clara.'

'I think it does...' I reply, suddenly feeling less guilty for leaving Noah behind.

Wearing a tiny orange playsuit with a pair of matching neon sandals and a huge straw hat, Gina comes to a stop in front of us and jangles her impressive collection of bracelets.

'Crack open the bubbles!' She sings, spinning around on the spot. 'This holiday starts right now!'

Pushing her way into the apartment, Gina makes a beeline for the fridge and plucks a bottle of fizz from the rack.

'The cab will be here in thirty minutes!' I giggle, hopping onto a stool as Gina grabs a selection of glasses from the cabinet.

'Exactly!' She replies, cheering as the cork pops with a bang. 'We have loads of time!'

Not being convinced, I watch Oliver help a flustered Marc into the apartment with the cases.

'What the hell do you have in there?' Oliver asks, kicking a case with his foot and steadying himself on the doorframe. 'Madison?'

'I think the kids are the only things Gina *didn't* pack.' Panting for breath, Marc groans and pauses to regain his composure. 'I'm going to go back for the others...'

'There's more?' I exclaim, looking at the huge leopard print suitcases in shock.

'One simply cannot be expected to manage five whole days with just two suitcases, darling.' Gina teases, as she fills four glasses with pink bubbles.

'Of course not, *darling.*' Tapping my glass against hers, I take a sip and swoon at the taste. 'Why isn't Marc using the lift?'

'He's trying to get some last-minute cardio in.' She explains, rolling her eyes and checking out her reflection in the bottle. 'I've been teasing him about his *dad bod.*'

Hiding my smile behind my glass, I look up as Oliver joins us at the kitchen island.

'So, how does it feel to be child-free, Gina?' He asks, brushing back his hair and resting his elbows on the counter.

'A-ma-zing!' She immediately replies, beaming brightly. 'It feels absolutely bloody fantastic!'

'Aren't you going to miss them at all?' I ask, taking another sip of sparkling wine. 'Not even a little bit?'

'Miss them?' She cackles, adjusting her tanned cleavage. 'You've got to be kidding me! Those three gremlins are going to be causing havoc while we're away.' Pausing to refill her glass, Gina shakes her black bob. 'Anyway, it's about time Marc's parents stepped up to the plate. They're always dodging grandparent duties.'

'Fair enough...' I reply, stifling a giggle as Marc returns with two more cases and collapses onto the sofa.

Taking a cold glass over to him, I sit on the arm of the couch and laugh as he drains the contents in one swift gulp. Wearing a pink shirt with a pair of white jeans and his favourite Suave boots, Marc's conservative style looks worlds away from Gina's *I've just stepped off the beach* vibe. His dark hair is perfectly slicked back and his trademark rectangle glasses are perched on the edge of his nose, finishing the look perfectly.

As I stare at my good friend, a whole rush of memories come flooding back to me. Marc and I have been through so much together and these last two years have really tested the strength of our friendship. The stress of the difficult takeover of Suave hit us all hard, but no one more so than Marc. The tension in the office turned him into a monster and I did worry that the old Marc was gone for good. However, I am pleased to say the Marc we know and love is back and we are now closer than ever.

'I *need* this holiday.' Mark mumbles, leaning back onto the cushions. 'No spreadsheets, no conference calls and no training sessions. I just want to eat and sleep for five days straight...'

'Aren't you forgetting a few things?' Gina interrupts, waving her glass around merrily. 'Cocktails, sunbathing, dancing...'

As Gina reels off her itinerary for the holiday, I catch Oliver's eye and feel my stomach flip. The flutters that signal an awaiting adventure on the other side of a flight are back with a vengeance. Being too consumed with my guilt over leaving Noah behind I haven't allowed myself to properly look forward to this trip, but now the time has finally come to leave, sun and sand are all I can think about.

Twirling my fingers around the stem of the glass, I tune my focus back into the conversation.

'And don't forget swimming!' Gina adds, reaching for the bottle once more. 'You've been like Nemo since you learnt how to swim in Barbados!'

Marc scowls with embarrassment as we all burst into laughter.

'Do we have time for another?' He asks, in a desperate bid to change the subject.

Glancing up at the clock on the wall, I shake my head in response. 'I'm afraid not. Li and Vernon should be here any minute now. Bottoms up, guys!'

An adrenaline-fuelled buzz rushes around the room as the four of us hurriedly check we have our holiday essentials in place. Satisfied that our passports and boarding passes are safely tucked away in the zipped compartment of my handbag, I clear away the used glasses and wait for the others to gather their belongings.

'Everyone ready?' Oliver asks, as Marc carries the last of the suitcases into the lobby.

A chorus of cheers rings around the group as I frantically ensure all the windows are locked. Casting a final glance around the apartment, I grab my keys and shoot Gina a frown as she hangs back from the others.

'Why are you walking like that?' I ask, watching her waddle out of the apartment like a duck with a bad case of trapped wind.

Popping a button on her playsuit, Gina points to a hidden bottle of wine and smiles mischievously.

'Gina! How old are you? Fifteen?' I scold, reaching into her playsuit and confiscating the offending fizz. 'If you want more alcohol you can buy it at the airport.'

Dumping the wine in the fridge where it belongs, I lock the door and slip the keys into my handbag.

'That's your first strike!' Gina grumbles haughtily, fastening her playsuit and deliberately leaving one too many buttons open. 'There's to be no *mothering* on this holiday.'

'I wasn't mothering!' I protest, linking my arm through hers as we follow the rest of the gang to the lift. 'But there's no point in bringing wine to the airport as you can't take liquids through security. And if you tried to drink it in the car it would probably spill...'

Holding up her hand to silence me mid-sentence, Gina stops in her tracks as Oliver and Marc step into the lift.

'That is your second strike.' She curses. 'One more and you won't be getting on that damn plane with us.'

A giggle bubbles in the back of my throat as I pretend to zip my lips together. 'Point taken.'

Flashing me the thumbs-up sign, Gina drags me into the lift and we immediately start to travel towards the ground floor. Turning to check out my skinny jeans and camisole combo in the mirror, I can't help but smile when I realise how funny we look. All dressed in our *we're going on holiday* outfits, we have officially become those adults who are desperately trying to recapture their youth and strangely, that makes me very happy.

Being in my thirties is fabulous and being a mother is even better, but a tiny part of me misses being a twenty-something young woman. There's something so magical about being in your twenties. To be footloose and fancy-free is a gift we so often take for granted in our younger years, but once that freedom is gone, it is extremely difficult to claw back. Of course, I don't resent getting older and I take each birthday as a huge accomplishment, but the idea of rediscovering my old self, even just for a few days, ignites a spark inside me that has been missing for so long.

Without warning the lift doors spring open, bringing my train of thought to a swift stop. Grabbing my suitcase, I leave the others to chat in the foyer and lead the way outside. My eyes narrow as they adjust to the bright light and I automatically dive into my handbag for my sunglasses.

Pausing for the others to catch up, I wave my arms around in the air as I see Lianna and Vernon in a minibus to my left. Immediately spotting me, Li leans across the driver's lap and presses his horn repeatedly.

'*Shh!*' I hiss, as passers-by stop to see what all the fuss is about. 'People are looking!'

Coming to a stop in front of the minibus, I smile broadly as Vernon pulls open the door.

'Hey!' He says with a grin, holding out his hand to help me inside. 'Ready to take on Mykonos?'

'You bet I am!' I reply, raising my eyebrows at his Hawaiian shirt. 'You do know that Greece isn't in Hawaii, don't you?'

'Of course, I do!' He adjusts his Panama hat and jumps down onto the pavement to grab my suitcase. 'What the hell was I supposed to wear? A toga?'

'I think you'd suit a toga.' I say teasingly. 'It would totally set off your dreadlocks.'

Vernon laughs and bats my arm playfully as I clamber over the seats. Holding onto the headrest to steady myself, I gasp as Lianna turns around to face me. Her usually blonde hair is now an icy shade of silver. Random streaks of pink, purple and blue run through her waves like a rainbow as she fluffs up her hair with her fingers.

'Your hair looks incredible!' I gush, dropping down onto the seat next to her and reaching out to touch her platinum mane. 'You look like a unicorn!'

'Do you like it?' Moving her head back and forth, she holds up a few stands of lilac and lets them fall back down. 'I was at the salon after our video call last night and I realised that my hair has been every single shade on the colour wheel.'

I nod along, recalling the many hair colours Lianna has rocked over the past few years.

'So...' She continues, looking at her reflection in the window. 'I thought, why not have all of them at the same time? I was a little worried I might look more like a unicorn vomited on me rather than an actual unicorn, but I think it's turned out alright.'

Gaping at her new style in awe, I catch a glimpse of my boring dark curls and make a mental note to visit the hairdresser when we return.

'I love it! Noah has been obsessed with unicorns lately…' My voice trails off as I spot a bottle of bubbly at her feet with a straw in the neck. 'What the hell is that?'

Before she can reply, the door closes with a bang as the rest of the gang jump into the minibus and take their seats.

'All aboard?' The driver shouts above the chatter.

'Yes!' We all yell in unison, as the vehicle slowly pulls away from the kerb.

'Who wants a drink?' Li asks, holding the bottle of fizz in the air.

'You spill that and you pay for the valet!' The driver grumbles, turning up the music to drown out the sound of Gina's cheers.

With a quick reassurance to the driver that she will be very careful, Lianna proceeds to pass the bottle around the group.

'Come on, guys! We're not on an 18-30s holiday!' Holding my head in my hands, I open my mouth to say something more, but a quick scowl from Gina makes me change my mind.

'Weren't those holidays just the best?' Gina muses, taking out the straw and swigging straight from the bottle. 'Ibiza, 1999. Now *that* was a holiday to remember…'

A wistful silence falls over the group as we all wonder what went down on Gina's infamous Ibiza trips.

'Ibiza has been my favourite holiday destination so far, hands down.' Draping her legs across Marc's lap, Gina sighs wistfully. 'What about you, Li? Barbados?'

'Barbados isn't exactly a holiday destination for us, it's our second home, but it's definitely our favourite place.' Lianna says with a fond smile. 'Isn't it, Vern?'

'It certainly is.' Vernon nods and wraps his spare arm around Lianna's shoulders.

Looking at the two of them together, my heart swells as I recall our trip to Barbados to meet Vernon for the very first time. What started as a typical holiday with the Lakes soon transpired into Lianna and Vernon tying the knot and it was the most beautiful wedding you could ever imagine.

'What has been *our* favourite holiday?' I ask Oliver, who is squashed between Marc and Vernon like a sardine. 'Mexico?'

'Mexico?' He repeats, raising his eyebrows. 'I suppose seeing you hurl on my mom's boots was pretty memorable.'

Laughter titters around the minibus and I blush in response. 'Not that part...'

'Wasn't Mexico where you bumped into Oliver's crazy ex?' Li asks, taking the wine bottle back from Gina.

'Erica was not an ex!' Oliver corrects, in a voice that makes his statement crystal clear. 'That woman was insane.'

'Maybe Orlando was our favourite holiday.' I mumble, my mind drifting back to wild roller coasters and the best cheeseburgers I have ever tasted.

A frown appears on Oliver's face and I immediately know why. As time has gone by, we can now laugh over our infamous trip to Mexico and our encounter with Erica, but any mention of Janie's ex-boyfriend, Paulie, is strictly off-limits.

'Who's to say *this* holiday won't be your favourite?' Gina says excitedly, a playful glint in her eye. 'This could be the holiday to top all holidays...'

'She's right.' Marc adds teasingly, shooting Lianna a wink. 'Maybe this will be an *extra special* holiday.'

I look over at Li as she giggles into the bottle of wine and frowns in confusion.

'What are you talking about?' Oliver asks, obviously as clueless as I am. 'Seriously, what's going on?'

Seemingly speaking on behalf of the others, Vernon leans forward in his seat and fixes his gaze on Oliver. 'We have a bet going.'

The driver takes a sharp right and I hold on to the railing overhead.

'A bet on what?' Oliver replies uneasily.

'The four of us...' Vernon continues, a silly smirk on his face as he points at Gina, Marc and Lianna. 'We have a bet that Stelios is going to propose to Janie.'

'Lordy halleluiah.' Oliver curses, shaking his head at Vernon in disbelief. 'Well, I'm going to save you all some time and money by telling you it isn't going to happen.'

'It better happen!' Gina yells. 'I've got a twenty riding on Janie having a ring on her finger by the end of the trip!'

I inhale sharply and glance over at Oliver. Knowing his hatred of Stelios is deep-rooted, I'm very aware of just how much this innocent bet is going to get under his skin.

'I have twenty on it *not* happening.' Lianna says softly, giving Oliver's arm a reassuring squeeze. 'Don't sweat it. I'm in your corner.'

'There are no corners!' Batting her hand away, Oliver forces himself to laugh and shakes his head. 'It isn't happening. *Period.*'

Trying not to laugh, I lean towards Vernon and lower my voice to a whisper. 'What do you have on it?'

'Clara!' Oliver cries, sounding completely appalled. 'Stop stoking the fire!'

'I'm just curious!' I reply, looking around the minibus. 'Who is down for a proposal?'

To Oliver's disgust, Vernon and Gina raise their hands in the air.

'Marc's with me.' Lianna says, giving him a high-five. 'We're going with no proposal.'

'Okay...' Plucking the bottle of fizz from Li, I take a big swig and clear my throat. 'How much can I bet on *Janie* proposing to *him?*'

Chapter 4

Smiling apologetically at the prissy air stewardess, who is desperately trying to squash Gina's mammoth collection of duty-free into the overhead lockers, I fasten my seatbelt and get comfortable. Despite my numerous warnings, Gina went completely crazy in the shops and came away with no less than ten bags of useless tat, resulting in her having to pay a fortune to bring her excess baggage onboard the aircraft.

With a final shove the air stewardess finally closes the locker, causing Gina to whoop raucously in the row behind me. The time she spent at the perfume counter has resulted in Gina smelling like a thirteen-year-old girl on her way to a One Direction concert and unsurprisingly, no one wanted to be her neighbour on the plane. Not that she's complaining, having an entire row of seats to herself appears to suit Gina just fine.

Peeking between the seats, I watch Gina flip through the in-flight magazine as the others chat about their plans for the trip. Joyous smiles are plastered on their faces and I automatically grin back. Being excited is a great feeling, but watching your friends when they're excited is even better. In the same way that giving a gift releases more endorphins than receiving one, hearing the laughter of my friends makes me deliriously happy.

Gina's cackle sets off Lianna's high-pitched giggle and within seconds, the guys are all laughing, too. This trip was worth it for this moment alone. After all, a holiday isn't about the expensive hotel rooms and materialistic keepsakes. It's about the memories that etch onto your heart and stay with you forever.

As I look on, my eyelids suddenly become heavy and I snuggle down into my seat, yawning lazily. The vast amount of fizz we consumed in the airport lounge is starting to take effect, causing me to feel incredibly sleepy. Allowing my eyes to close, I pull the complimentary blanket up to my chin and groan as Lianna appears beside me.

'We're playing Jenga!' She exclaims, dropping down onto my lap. 'Come on! I want you on my team.'

'Do I have to?' Letting out a whimper, I silently curse her as I kiss goodbye to my nap. 'I could really do with a little downtime.'

'Don't be such a party pooper!' Li scowls back at me and hiccups loudly. 'We're on holiday!'

'Right now, we're on the tarmac at Heathrow Airport.' I correct, not realising until it's too late that I do, in fact, sound like a fun sponge. 'Sorry. I'm just exhausted. You guys play without me...'

My words fade into silence as an announcement floods into the cabin.

'Ladies and gentleman, this is your pilot speaking. I am afraid we are in for a bit of a delay. Due to unforeseen circumstances, a flight destined for Manchester has been rerouted to Heathrow. We're currently working to clear the traffic and we should be on our way to Mykonos as soon as possible. Your cabin crew will update you with more information as and when it comes in. Apologies for the inconvenience.'

A groan echoes around the aircraft and I frown at Lianna when I realise she's beaming brightly.

'Why do you look so happy?' I mutter, grabbing a safety card from the pocket in front of me. 'We're going to be stuck here for bloody ages!'

'Exactly!' She replies, reaching down and unclipping my seatbelt. 'Now you have no excuse not to join in!'

Rolling my eyes, I grudgingly allow her to drag me out of my seat. 'Fine, but once we set off, I'm definitely sleeping!'

Quickly tidying my hair, I follow Li along the aisle and join the others by the window. Luckily, the business class cabin is completely empty and therefore we're able to enjoy the entire area to ourselves.

'I've recruited another one for Jenga!' Lianna says cheerfully, tipping the wooden blocks onto the tray in front of Marc. 'Let's do this!'

'You will have to put that away very shortly.' The air hostess grumbles curtly, frowning at us as she kicks Lianna's bags under the seat in front of her.

'The pilot just explained that we're in for a bit of a delay.' Gina replies with a smile. 'But don't worry, we'll make sure it's all packed away before we take off. In the meantime, is there any way we could get some drinks?'

Adjusting her navy blazer, the air stewardess puckers her brow. 'There shall be no beverage service until fifteen minutes after take-off. Until then, enjoy your... *game.*'

Turning on her heel she marches down the walkway, leaving a trail of musty perfume in her wake.

'I'll take that as a *no*.' Gina replies cheekily, sticking her tongue out. 'Who rattled her cage?'

Trying not to laugh, I cover my smile with a Jenga block as the air stewardess fires Gina a glare.

'Well, as there's no alcohol on offer, whoever causes the tower to fall has to up their bet.' Vernon says, stacking the wooden blocks on Marc's tray. 'That should make it more interesting.'

Oliver curses under his breath as the rest of the gang hoot in agreement.

'Alright!' Marc claps his hands together and places the final block on the tower. 'Who's going first?'

* * *

Feeling the ground rumble beneath my feet, I stir in my sleep and slowly peel open my eyes. My mouth is drier than the desert and my bum is numb from sitting on a seatbelt buckle, but catching a glimpse of the azure water out of the window makes none of that matter.

Pressing my nose against the glass, I squint as the sun beams down onto the wing of the plane, almost blinding me with a bright light. Wispy clouds dance across the sky, smattering the sheet of blue with cotton candy swirls as we glide past at high-speed. Narrowing my eyes, I spot land in the distance and silently squeal as Mykonos twinkles back at me, welcoming me to my new home for the next five days.

Taking a deep breath, I stretch out my legs and listen to the happy chatter that is drifting out from the row behind me. At my last check, Jenga bets placed on

Stelios proposing to Janie were shockingly high. I dread to think what outlandish figures they are throwing around now. Amazingly, despite Oliver's initial disgust at the wager, he eventually gave in and placed a big fat bet on the engagement *not* taking place. In his words, there was no way on this planet that his mother was marrying a creep like Stelios, so he might as well make some money out of it.

Finally tearing my eyes away from the glistening ocean, I tap the screen in front of me and feel a rush of adrenaline as I discover we are just thirty minutes away from our destination. The tiny icon moves at a snail's pace across the map, giving the illusion that we have almost stopped mid-air. Completely mesmerised by the display, I almost don't hear my name being called behind me.

My seat creaks as I rest my chin on the headrest and smile at the view in front of me. Lianna and Vernon are huddled under a blanket watching a movie, Marc and Oliver are playing cards on the pull-out tray between them and Gina is merrily swigging from yet *another* glass of wine.

'You're finally awake!' Gina cheers, almost spilling her chardonnay. 'Guys! Clara's up!'

One by one, my friends turn to look at me and promptly start to clap as I step out into the aisle to give my legs a proper stretch.

'Finally!' Oliver says with a grin. 'You've missed all the fun! It's all been going on back here!'

Judging by the smiles on everyone's faces I have indeed missed out on the jovialities, but the chance to sleep for a few hours was just too alluring. These days, any opportunity of catching forty winks is just too irresistible to turn down. My mother always jokes that you know you're a parent when your deepest fantasies are about being in bed alone, without an alarm clock or a demanding child to wake you and I'm not ashamed to admit that an empty bed is all my heart desires.

As I am fantasizing about freshly laundered bedding the plane suddenly jolts, causing me to hold on to the seat in front to steady myself.

'We shall shortly be starting our descent into Mykonos.
Could all passengers please return to their seats and fasten their seatbelts.'

Gina squeals and throws her arms into the air, much to the disdain of the grumpy air stewardess who slips out from behind the curtain and instructs us all to sit down like a strict headmistress. Not wanting another scolding, I wave to the others and retreat to my seat.

Noticing the *fasten seatbelt* sign illuminate overhead, I check my belongings are all safely zipped into my handbag and watch the steady stream of people race along the walkway in a last-minute dash to the toilet. Each one of the passengers has that beautiful pre-holiday glow about them. The anticipation of landing on Greek soil is hanging thickly in the air. You can almost see it twirling around the many happy holidaymakers, creating a sparkling atmosphere as we count down to landing.

Hearing Gina and Oliver light-heartedly argue over Stelios's hidden agenda in asking us to Mykonos, I turn my attention back to the window as we start to descend. Feeling my stomach flutter once more, I cross my legs as the lights dim on the aircraft, signalling that we're about to land. The slight trembling beneath me quickly escalates to a forceful rumble, until the wheels finally hit the ground with a bump.

Happy chatter rings around the aircraft as passengers scramble to gather their luggage in a desperate attempt to start their holiday. Looking back at my friends, I smile widely and unclip my seatbelt. For us, this trip might not be the traditional package holiday, but with sun, sea and sand on offer, hopefully, it will be just as fun…

Chapter 5

The intense sunshine blares down on my bare shoulders as I step out of the airport and revel in the incredibly warm rays. I can almost feel the vitamin D as it is absorbed through my pale skin, giving me the boost I have been craving for so very long.

Completely losing myself in the moment, I snap to attention as I hear Gina's heels clacking on the tarmac behind me. After making the most of the complimentary drinks on the plane, it's no surprise she's looking a little worse for wear. With her black hair in disarray and the straps on her playsuit hanging dangerously low, she looks like a teenager doing the walk of shame, not a married mother-of-three who's just stepped off a business class flight.

'Do you want some water?' I ask, reaching into my handbag for the bottle of Evian I stuffed in there earlier.

'Only if there's gin in it.' Reluctantly accepting the bottle, Gina raises it to her lips and grimaces.

Noticing the tip of her nose is already turning red, I hand her some sun lotion I picked up in the airport. 'You might want to stand in the shade. Hangovers and sunstroke go together like fish fingers and chocolate.'

'Fish fingers and chocolate? I'm sure I've given that to the kids in the past.' Gina jokes, ignoring my advice and joining the others by the side of the road.

My heart pangs at the mention of the kids and I try to shake it off. I only said goodbye to Noah this morning and I'm already missing his chubby little cheeks like crazy.

'I think we're going to need three cabs.' I say to Oliver, in an attempt to distract myself from the subject of Noah. 'Maybe four, given Gina's luggage.'

Hearing the word *cab*, Gina automatically wobbles towards the taxi rank with the bottle of water glued to her lips. Her legs tremble like jelly as she clumsily puts one foot in front of the other. Suddenly immensely grateful to have slept through her drinking marathon, I take a moment to relish in having a clear head and inwardly give myself a high-five.

Just as the rest of us start to follow in Gina's footsteps, a ping from Oliver's pocket causes him to hang back. Watching him dig out the handset and squint at the screen, I shield my eyes from the sun and take a step towards him.

'Who is it?' I ask, resting my spare hand on my suitcase.

'My mom...' A frown creeps onto his face as he studies the text message closely.

'Hold up!' He shouts to the others, who immediately stop and turn around. 'Stelios has sent a car to collect us. Apparently, the driver is already here.'

'Do you know where, exactly?' Marc asks, wiping a bead of sweat from his brow and scouring the area for our ride.

Oliver shakes his head and slips the phone back into his pocket.

'I need to get out of these boots before I melt!' Unbuttoning his shirt, Marc fans himself with a Mykonos guide and leans against his suitcase.

'Well, you did choose to travel in bloody boots!' Lianna teases, pointing to her sandals and shorts smugly. 'Where did you think we were going? Alaska?'

Ignoring her comments, Marc points to a white limousine that has pulled into the car park across the road. Knowing without asking that this pimped-out limousine belongs to Stelios, I smile at Li as Vernon and Marc make their way towards the luxury car.

'Trust *him* to send something so extravagant.' Oliver complains, scowling and grabbing our cases. 'I mean, a limo? Is that really necessary?'

'Stelios travels *everywhere* by limousine.' I reply gently, attempting to gloss over the fact that it is indeed excessive. 'He owns an entire fleet of the things, so why would he send anything else?'

Oliver swears under his breath and I pretend I haven't heard him as we follow the others across the road.

'Can you please at least *try* to be happy on this holiday?' I ask, pushing my sunglasses into my hair. 'I understand your feelings towards Stelios, I really do, but just give the guy a chance for your mum's sake.'

Folding his arms like a stubborn child, Oliver turns away and stares into the distance.

'If you can't do it for your mum, then do it for me. Just enjoy this for the adventure that it is.' Turning his head back to face me, I stare into his eyes intently. 'Can you do that for me, please?'

He mumbles something I don't quite catch and I cup my hands around my ears. 'I'm sorry?'

'I said, *I will try*.' He replies through gritted teeth, manipulating his lips into a strained smile.

'That'll do.' Trying not to laugh at his forced happy face, I entwine my fingers with his as we walk across the car park to the waiting limousine.

Handing our cases to the suited driver, who is wearing a name badge labelled *Calix*, I offer him a smile and hop into the vehicle.

'*Oww!*' I yell, as I bang my toe against one of Gina's many suitcases. 'What are these doing in here?'

Poking his head into the limo, Calix smiles apologetically. 'I am very sorry, but the cases are... too many. They will not all fit in the back.'

Rubbing my throbbing toe, I screw up my nose as Oliver slides onto the seat next to me.

'Who brings this much luggage on such a short trip?' I hiss. 'Is Gina planning on staying here or something?'

Happily snapping a picture of Vernon and Marc on her phone, Li glances back at me and frowns. 'Where *is* Gina?'

Looking around the group, I notice the same look of confusion appear on everyone's faces.

'She's around here somewhere.' Marc says uncertainly, looking out of the tinted window and scouring the car park. 'She was right in front of me when we were at the taxi rank.'

'She didn't get into a taxi, did she?' Li gasps, as we all turn to look at Marc.

'Oh, no...' Jumping out of the limo, Marc runs across the car park at record speed, dodging the many tourists as he goes.

I watch him dash from taxi to taxi, before pulling open one of the doors and reappearing with an intoxicated Gina over his shoulder.

'She did!' Vernon laughs loudly and whips out his phone to take a picture. 'She actually got into a cab!'

Panting for breath, Marc flashes us the thumbs-up sign as he carries Gina across the hot tarmac like a sleeping toddler. Oliver is the first to let out a cheer and the rest of us swiftly join in. Clapping and whooping at the top of our lungs, we erupt into hysterics when Marc finally makes it back to the limo.

'Is she okay?' Calix asks, a look of alarm washing across his face as Marc places a sozzled Gina onto the back seats.

'She's fine.' Propping her into a sitting position, Marc takes a moment to steady his breathing before clapping Calix on the back. 'She's just had a little too much...'

Making a drinking sign with his hand, Marc nods knowingly as Calix laughs.

'Oh! I see!' Giggling into his collar, Calix quickly composes himself before ushering Marc into the vehicle. 'Don't you worry. I shall have you with Mr Christopoulos in no time at all.'

With a final friendly grin, Calix shuts the door and hops into the driver's seat.

Hearing the engine fire up, I squeeze Oliver's knee and smile when he beams back at me. Relieved to see he's making the effort, I rest my head on his chest as the limousine slowly purrs away from the airport.

The arid landscape scrolls past the window, making a stark difference to the skyscrapers of London we're all accustomed to. Breathing deeply, I look up at the sheet of blue sky stretching out as far as the eye can see and instantly feel a million miles away from home.

'Does anyone actually know where we're going?' Lianna asks, taking a compact mirror out of her handbag and checking her makeup.

I shake my head and look at the others, who appear as clueless as I am. 'We've seen photographs of Stelios's home online, but I have no idea where it is.'

'I still say we should have booked our own accommodation.' Oliver says matter-of-factly. 'Why would we want to stay with him when we could've just made a hotel reservation?'

'Yeah...' Lianna replies with a frown. 'Why would we possibly want to stay in Stelios's fabulous mansion over a mediocre hotel down the road?'

'Besides, we *have* to stay with Stelios.' Vernon says jokingly, adjusting his hat. 'We want to be around when he asks for your mother's hand in marriage. No way are we missing that!'

A laugh titters around the limo and even Oliver joins in, but before I can make a joke of my own, Gina groans in her sleep.

'How much did she have to drink?' I ask Marc, who gives her a swift nudge in the ribs.

'Everything!' Lianna answers on his behalf. 'Wine, vodka, rum. The list is endless! You name it and she drank it.'

My parental instincts suddenly kick in and I scour my carry-on luggage for more water.

'Maybe we should get Gina some coffee or something. We can't turn up with her in this state.' I mumble, plucking a packet of paracetamol from my purse. 'It doesn't exactly make a good impression, does it? Stelios *is* a client of ours. I don't think Owen would be too impressed if he could see her right now.'

'Stelios lives with *Janie!*' Li chuckles. 'He will see this kind of behaviour all day long.'

I feel Oliver tense in his seat and I squeeze his hand.

'Still, I think we should try and sober her up a bit before we arrive.' Crouching down, I walk towards Calix and tap on the privacy screen. 'Excuse me?'

Lowering the partition, Calix turns down the radio and flashes me a huge grin. 'Yes?'

'Would it possible to stop at a coffee shop on the way? I think my friend could do with some... *fresh air*.' Pointing at Gina, I raise my eyebrows and hope he can read between the lines.

'No problem. I understand.' Hitting the indicator, he takes a sharp left and presses his foot on the accelerator. 'I take you for the best coffee on the island. Just sit back, relax and let me look after you...'

Chapter 6

Kicking off my sandals, I drag a wicker chair out of the shade and collapse into its plush cushioned seat. The heat from the sun is even more powerful than it was before, making me feel as though I've just slipped into the most wonderful bubble bath. Taking a deep breath, I look out over the calm water and feel every muscle in my body start to relax. A slight breeze wraps around me as I watch a couple of young children collecting stones on the pebbled beach below. Their cries of joy hang in the air, causing passing people to stop and smile as they stroll along the shore, enjoying their own holiday.

After the early start this morning and a rather lengthy delay on the aircraft, I am beyond relieved to finally be relaxing in the sunshine. Being on holiday is, of course, fabulous, but the journey to get there can sometimes be more stressful than you anticipate. *Especially* when you are travelling with a woman approaching forty who is determined to relive her teenage years...

Looking to my left, I lift my sunglasses and steal a glance at a very hungover Gina. Sprawled out on a double sunbed, she holds a wet flannel against her head while cradling a hot coffee. Her drunken smile has vanished and in its place is a scowl that screams, *I have a raging headache and a mouth like a dusty flip-flop.*

'How are you feeling?' I ask, sensing from the glare she replies with the answer is *absolutely dreadful*. 'That bad, huh?'

She manages a curt nod, before pulling a towel over her head and rolling onto her side. Following Calix's advice, we ordered Gina a Greek coffee and a rather strange-looking vinegar concoction. Apparently, Calix's ancestors swore by the random vinegar-based drink to cure a hangover, but judging by the copious amounts of heaving Gina did while trying to throw it back, I'm not holding my breath.

Leaving her to recuperate for a while longer, I push myself up and wander over to Lianna, who has been playing photographer on the terrace for the past thirty minutes.

'Isn't this place adorable?' She gushes, leaning over the railing and snapping at the beautiful scene with her phone. 'I could stay here forever.'

Tucking my hair behind my ears, I look at my surroundings and sigh. 'It is pretty spectacular…'

Being ever so accommodating, Calix took us on a detour to the most fabulous coffee shop I've ever seen. Well, to call it a *coffee shop* isn't really fair. Set in the cliffside overlooking a beautiful beach, Azure is a coffee shop and then some. The iconic white building features an open-air eating area, with more swanky chairs and quirky bean bags than you could ever imagine. Charming lanterns are scattered around the place, making me long to be here at sunset to watch the waves by candlelight. A long bar made of driftwood creates the perfect centrepiece and is surrounded by everyone from local elderly couples, to tourists enjoying a true taste of Mykonos.

'You like it?' Calix asks, smiling proudly as he stands by the limo.

'No, I *love* it!' Tearing myself away from the spectacular view, I join him in the shade. 'Thank you so much for bringing us here.'

'It is no problem.' Taking a bottle of water from the limo, Calix wipes his brow on his forearm. 'Azure is my favourite place to visit when I need some rest and how do you say... *renovate?*'

'Rejuvenate.' I correct with a grin. 'It really is a fabulous place, but I'm sure taking inebriated women for coffee to sober up isn't in your job description.'

Calix's brown eyes crinkle into his smile as he shakes his head. 'Actually, in my job description, *nothing* is out of bounds.'

'Nothing?' I reply, watching Gina curl up into a ball under her towel.

'*Nothing.*' Calix lowers his voice to a whisper and leans towards me. 'Whatever Stelios wants, Stelios gets. It is in my job description to make that happen, at all costs.'

Dreading to think what outrageous tasks Stelios instructs Calix to do, I respond with a nervous laugh and excuse myself to go in search of my husband. Squeezing past a young family, who are enjoying an enormous plate of meze dishes, I follow the sound of Oliver's voice through the bar.

Eventually finding the guys playing cards with a friendly bartender, I dodge a snoozing cat and make my way over to them. With beer bottles in their hands and their t-shirts tied loosely around their waists, they look like they started their holiday a long time ago. Pausing by a pillar, I take a moment to study them from afar and remark at the stark difference in Oliver.

His deep laugh echoes around the room and I automatically grin. In just a few hours, his eyes appear brighter, his smile seems deeper and his shoulders are no longer tight with stress.

Catching his eye, I raise my hand in acknowledgement and walk over to them.

'Hey!' Oliver says, pulling me onto his lap and kissing my warm cheek. 'How's Gina doing over there?'

'Erm...' I screw up my nose and look back at where Gina is currently snoozing. 'Just give her another ten minutes.'

Marc laughs into his beer bottle and squints at his snoring wife. 'Yeah, just let her sleep it off. She'll be fine.'

Tactfully leaving us to talk, the bartender places a bowl of exotic nuts on the counter and disappears to serve another customer.

'When Gina said she intended to relive her youth on this vacation, she wasn't joking, was she?' Vernon remarks, slipping a crisp note beneath his empty bottle. 'What's next on her list? Skinny-dipping and wet t-shirt contests?'

'I think today has been more than enough to prove she isn't as young as she thinks she is.' I reply, reaching for Oliver's beer. 'Trying to act like a teenager is the quickest way to realise you're not one. She'll probably sleep for the rest of the trip.'

'Do you want to place a bet on that?' Marc chuckles.

'I think one bet is quite enough for this holiday, don't you?' Sliding to my feet, I adjust my shorts and twist my hair into a ponytail. 'On that note, we should probably make a move. Janie will be wondering where we are.'

Nodding in agreement, the guys swiftly finish their drinks and say their goodbyes to the bartender before following me through the bar. My feet burn on the hot tiles as I lead the way over to where Gina is sleeping and prod her sunbed with my foot. Not getting a response, I bend down and slowly lift her towel.

'Don't look at me.' Covering her eyes with her hands, Gina stumbles as she pushes herself into a sitting position. 'Nobody talk to me.'

'We're going to set off now.' Marc says gently, holding out his hand to help her to her feet. 'Do you think you can make it the rest of the way without hurling, or do you want another cocktail for the road?'

'Absolutely not.' Roughly shoving on her sunglasses, Gina stands up and steadies herself on Marc's arm. 'I don't want to hear the word *cocktail* for the remainder of this holiday.'

Trying not to laugh, I rub her back reassuringly and move away when she quickly shakes my hand off. 'Add *no touching* to the list. Nobody look at me, speak to me, or touch me.'

'What happened to Ibiza, 1999?' Oliver teases, winking at Marc as he tries to comfort her.

Not bothering to respond, Gina wraps the towel around her body and gingerly wobbles over to the waiting limousine.

'I don't think we need to worry about Gina becoming a holiday rep, put it that way.' Lianna jokes, reaching for Vernon's hand as we watch Gina scramble into the back of the limo. 'Mykonos One – Gina Nil...'

* * *

Fifteen minutes and a whole lot of air-conditioning-hogging later, Calix indicates left and pulls up outside a set of impressive iron gates. The sporadic breaks in the railings provide a glimpse of the magnificent property behind it, making my stomach flip with excitement. An imposing fence surrounds the expansive plot, completely shielding the prestigious villa from the winding road.

Straining my neck for a closer look, I watch in awe as Calix leans out of the limousine window and presses a button on the intercom. Almost immediately, the gates swing open and the vehicle effortlessly glides into the grounds. The white mansion is unbelievably bright under the strong rays of sunshine, causing all six of us to reach for our sunglasses. Acres of perfectly manicured lawn stretch out around the snaking path, which leads to a carport holding several stretch limousines identical to this one.

I've seen so many photographs of Stelios's home online, but viewing it for real has left me completely lost for words. I simply cannot believe *this* is where Janie has been for the past twelve months. Of course, Stelios's wealth isn't a secret and I completely expected to be impressed by his home, but this is on a whole new level altogether. It seems there's money and then there's *money*. Stelios's billionaire status is evident everywhere you look and it's almost difficult to take it all in.

Feeling Calix bring the limo to a stop, we clamber out onto the path and look up at the impressive building. Judging by the shocked expression on

Oliver's face, it seems the realisation of Stelios's wealth is finally sinking in for all of us. Too stunned to speak, we stand frozen to the spot as Calix promptly unloads the suitcases with the help of two assistants, who seem to have magically appeared from nowhere.

Slipping my hands into my pockets, I watch as Calix whispers into his headset and two burly security guards step out from behind the pillars by the front door. Instantly recognising them as the pair of heavies who accompany Stelios on his London trips, I offer them a nervous smile as they come to a halt in front of the limo.

After giving us a quick once-over, they turn back to the wooden door and slowly walk up the stone steps in silence.

'What's going on?' Li discreetly murmurs into my ear. 'Where's Stelios?'

As if answering her question, the doors swing open with a flourish to reveal a very giddy Stelios. Wearing a crisp white shirt, which is hanging open to expose his impressive amount of chest hair, he holds open his arms as he races down the steps. His teeth are littered with gold and his bouffant hair is perfectly combed over, emulating a retro porn star.

'My family!' Stelios sings, throwing his arms around my neck and squeezing me tightly. 'My family have arrived!'

Hoping that *family* translates into *work colleagues I am on a first-name basis with* in Greek, I hug him back as he shifts his focus to Lianna. Clearly not bothered by his overly friendly greeting, Lianna giggles as he delights in complimenting her new hair.

Noticing Oliver freeze as Stelios reaches up and gives him the eager beaver treatment too, I wait until everyone has been greeted before speaking up.

'Thank you so much for inviting us to your home, Stelios.' I gush, as he embraces me once again. 'It's an honour to be here...'

'Nonsense!' Stelios yells joyously, cutting me off with a cheer. 'My home, is *your* home. You are all my family now!'

Nervous laughter titters around the group and I feel Oliver tense next to me.

'Please, come with me!' Clicking his fingers at the cases, Stelios nods as they're swiftly ushered away by Calix and his helpers. 'I show you the way...'

Tracing Stelios's footsteps, I look at Oliver as Vernon tugs on his sleeve.

'Better get that money ready, Morgan.' He jokes quietly, making sure to keep his voice low. 'This engagement is in the bag!'

Oliver attempts to stop himself from smiling as Vernon continues to wind him up.

'*My family! My family! My family!*' Vernon sings, clapping Oliver on the back. 'Say *hello* to your new stepdad, dude!'

Trying not to laugh, I bat Vernon on the arm as we jog up the steps and follow Stelios into the building. With Stelios's eccentric style and often garish choices of clothing, I was expecting his home to reflect exactly that. The truth is, this place has been designed with elegance, grace and heaps of class.

The neutral walls are complimented beautifully with touches of gold and bronze, in the form of various ostentatious ornaments and decorations. Heavy mirrors, which wouldn't look out of place in

Buckingham Palace, make the palatial entrance hall appear even bigger than it already is. Enormous bouquets of roses and bubbling water features fill the open space beautifully, providing the perfect finishing touch.

'Wait a minute...' Lianna hisses. 'Where's Janie?'

Pulling my brow into a frown, I look at Oliver expecting him to know the answer. Being so consumed with my admiration for Stelios's home, I hadn't realised the person we flew out here to see is missing.

'Where *is* Janie?' I repeat, intentionally raising my voice for Stelios to hear.

'My Janie is right here.' He babbles excitedly, signalling for us to keep walking. 'Don't you worry, my friends. I bring you to my Janie right now.'

Oliver's daggers burn into the side of my head at hearing Stelios label his mother *my Janie* twice in as many sentences and I pretend not to notice. Tugging my handbag onto my shoulder, I look up as we turn a corner and find ourselves in a narrow corridor. An intricate stained-glass door glistens at us in the distance as we continue to walk, sandwiched between Stelios and his minders. Not daring to look at Oliver, I chew the inside of my cheek anxiously as Stelios punches a code into a keypad and pushes open the door.

Glistening tiles welcome us into the room, leading to the most outstanding indoor swimming pool. A huge fountain spurts a foaming stream into the glittering water, making the sparkling black tiles appear deeper than the ocean. Lights resembling stars are sprinkled across the ceiling, giving the illusion we're actually on the beach at midnight and not indoors at midday.

Resisting the urge to dive straight in, I take a few steps to the left and squeal as Janie drifts into view. Wearing a tiny bikini, my crazy mother-in-law is sprawled out in a pink flamingo, with an elaborate cocktail glass in her hand. Her famous beehive is hanging loosely in delicate waves around her face and her mahogany tan is ten shades darker than the last time I saw her.

'Welcome to Mykonos!' She cackles, splashing her legs in the water and showering us in the process. 'Well, what you all waiting for? Get in here!'

Dipping a toe into the water, I turn around to ask Stelios where our cases are when I'm suddenly drenched by water. Wiping my eyes, my jaw drops open as I realise Li has jumped straight into the pool, fully clothed.

'*Lianna!*' I yell, watching her swim over to Janie in her tiny denim shorts. 'Aren't you waiting for your swimsuit?'

Remembering her swimsuit is the most inappropriate excuse for a swimming costume I have ever seen, I'm quietly glad when she ignores my question.

'I'm going for it.' Not hesitating, Vernon whips off his Hawaiian shirt and places his shoes neatly next to the steps. 'Who's with me?'

Quickly mimicking Vernon, Marc sheds everything but his shorts and removes his glasses. Without hesitation the pair of them dive into the water, quickly followed by Gina, who seems to have miraculously overcome her hangover at the sight of Stelios's magnificent pool.

Not wanting to be left out, I look at Oliver before stepping out of my sandals. The cheers of my friends egg me on as I take a deep breath before leaping into the unknown. Adrenaline rushes through my body as I hit the surface of the water and kick my legs frantically to stay afloat. Swimming across the mammoth pool, I join the others by Janie and reach up to give her a well overdue squeeze. The second my arms wrap around hers, I am reminded of just how much I have missed having her around. Her familiar perfume makes me feel weirdly emotional as we hug one another closely, neither one wanting to let go.

Finally tearing myself away, I turn around in the water as Janie clears her throat and fixes her gaze on Oliver.

'Son?' She says, a soft tone to her voice I haven't heard before. 'Are you joining us?'

My ears ring with adrenaline as Janie and Oliver lock eyes for the first time in a year. Identical expressions are glued to their faces as they stare at one another in silence. Shifting my gaze over to Stelios, I notice he is also holding his breath. As hard as Stelios has tried to pretend the tension between him and Oliver isn't there, I know Oliver's refusal to accept him in his life hurts Stelios a lot more than he would ever let you know.

Without making a sound, Oliver steps forward and allows himself to fall into the water. Clapping my hands together as he comes up for air, I feel my heart fill with pride. Despite him being a grown man, I am beyond proud of Oliver for putting his opinions to one side to please his mum, even if it is just for the time being. Whether you are four, fourteen or forty, sacrificing your own feelings for the sake of a loved one is always an action to be celebrated.

Shaking water out of his eyes, Oliver brushes his hair back before swimming over to Janie. Leaving the two of them to become reacquainted, the rest of us splash one another animatedly as Stelios watches on from the safety of the deck. Holding up a pizza-shaped float to avoid Marc's attempts to dunk me under the water, I catch Stelios smiling fondly.

'Are you coming in, Stelios?' I ask, abandoning my float and holding on to the edge of the pool.

'No.' Suddenly looking rather uneasy, Stelios fidgets with his hands as we all turn to look at him. 'I enjoy the pool at all times. This is *your* time to enjoy the pool...'

'Oh, come on.' I press, feeling a little sorry for him. 'Join us!'

After initially hesitating, Stelios nods and slowly makes for the steps, much to the delight of Janie. Pleased he has decided to join the party, I shoot him the thumbs-up sign as he reaches for the railing. Abruptly stopping halfway down the stairs, Stelios walks back onto the deck and shouts loudly in Greek. With a sudden burst of determination, he takes a running jump and bombs into the water like a small child.

Being very aware Stelios is pushing seventy, I cover my mouth with my hands as Janie shrieks in shock.

'What the hell are you doing?' She cries, shaking her head in disbelief as Stelios resurfaces. 'You're going to give yourself a damn heart attack!'

Throwing his arms into the air, Stelios sprays water over Janie as she beams back at him.

'And if so, my Janie, I would die a very happy man...'

Chapter 7

Stepping out of the shower, I reach for a towel and wrap myself up like a fluffy burrito. Despite only spending a slight amount of time in the sun, my skin feels warm and toasty as I wipe condensation from the mirror and reach for my moisturiser. Smothering my face with soothing aloe vera, I smile as the bright lights around the glass shine back on me, creating a halo effect around my reflection.

After our impromptu swim in Stelios's ocean, sorry, *pool*, earlier, Stelios instructed his chefs to cook up an array of mouth-watering snacks to whet our appetite for dinner this evening. While we dried our clothes on the outdoor terrace and enjoyed the most delicious canapés, Janie took great pleasure in filling us in on the last twelve months of her life.

It seems while the rest of us have been worrying about her antics over here, Janie's life has actually been quite serene. Apart from lounging by the pool and accompanying Stelios to business dinners, the only thing that tears her away from the villa are her weekly dates with Stelios's mum, Konstantina. From coffee dates at Azure to shopping trips around the local markets, from what I've heard, Janie has made a friend for life and been granted the royal stamp of approval in the process.

Astonishingly, it appears Konstantina genuinely adores Janie and just like the rest of the gang, I'm still trying to work out how that could possibly be. With her outlandish behaviour, crude language and refusal to act her age, Janie isn't exactly the woman a mother dreams of for her son. Although, I have to hand it to Janie, being with Stelios has really calmed her down and *not* made her go off the rails as we had anticipated.

Although he didn't say anything in response to Janie's revelations about her life here, I did notice Oliver was quietly surprised at the change in his mother. We were all concerned that having access to such an obscene amount of money would allow Janie to become even more intrepid than she already is, but if this initial meeting is anything to go by, Stelios has brought the best out in Janie and her in him.

'It feels so bizarre to be showering in the middle of the bedroom...' I muse, shaking all thoughts of Janie from my mind and abandoning my towel.

'And it's even more bizarre that I can't see you.' Walking over to the enormous booth, Oliver marvels at the privacy glass. 'You can see me, but I can't see you. How amazing is that?'

'It is pretty cool, but I wouldn't want one at home.' Stepping out of the cubicle, I drop down onto the cloud-like bed and pull open a drawer in search of the underwear I unpacked earlier. 'It makes a feel a little... *exposed.*'

'I'd totally have one!' Oliver replies energetically, as he walks around the bedroom with wide eyes. 'I'd have the whole interior of this place at our apartment!'

A slight twinkle plays on the corner of my mouth as I watch him speak. 'You would?'

'Yeah.' He says hesitantly, swapping his smile for a frown. 'Why are you looking at me like that?'

'No reason!' Realising I'm smiling manically, I clear my throat and reach for a dressing gown. 'I'm just so pleased you've decided to accept Stelios...'

'Accept Stelios?' He repeats, almost angrily. 'What the hell gave you that impression?'

Completely flummoxed by his response, I pause with my hands on my hips and wait for him to laugh. 'Are you joking?'

'Are *you* joking?' He replies, an edge to his voice I don't like.

'No...' Sitting back down on the bed, I laugh uncertainly. 'You seemed to be getting on so well just now. From where I was standing, it looked like you two were really bonding.'

'Clara, laughing at the guy's jokes and swimming in his pool does *not* mean I have accepted his relationship with my mother.' Oliver snaps, reaching behind the partition and turning on the shower.

'But you were getting along so well!' I stammer, saddened that I appear to have misread the signals. 'I don't understand.'

Letting out a scoff, he tugs his t-shirt over his head and steps into the glass cubicle. 'I've told you before and I will tell you again. This is purely a business trip. I will tolerate Stelios because we work with him, but that is all. That's where the pleasantries end...'

He turns on the taps and his voice becomes muffled by the sound of thundering water.

'If Owen wouldn't have insisted on me coming here, we wouldn't even be having this conversation.' Oliver continues. 'The reason I'm being nice is because *you* asked me to. There's nothing more to it!'

Staring at the glass box in the middle of the room, I suddenly feel rather uneasy.

'But can't you see how happy your mum is with him?' I press, not wanting to push him to the point where he loses his temper.

'My mom would be happy with a *pig* if it had a billion dollars in the bank.' He retorts. 'Who or where the money comes from is totally irrelevant.'

'I disagree. I think there's something very real and endearing about them.' Reaching for my cosmetic case, I take a seat at the marble dressing table and flick on the illuminating lights. 'My gut instinct is generally right and I, for one, think they're the real deal.'

'That's good for you, Clara, but I will *never* accept Stelios as my mom's partner.' Oliver yells, above the sound of the shower. 'Not now, not ever.'

'Well, I believe Stelios really cares about Janie and vice versa...' Starting to feel defensive over Stelios and Janie's relationship, I scowl at the cubicle and stick out my tongue.

Oliver shouts something I don't quite catch in response and I choose to ignore him. Stelios is taking us all out for dinner at one of his friend's restaurants this evening and I have just thirty minutes to make myself presentable. Diving into a swimming pool when you're fully clothed might seem like a fun idea at the time, but it also means you risk resurfacing like a kraken from the sea.

Attacking my face with various lotions and potions, I wonder how Gina is getting on in the next room. I don't know whether it was Calix's peculiar vinegar remedy or impulsively diving into Stelios's swimming pool earlier, but Gina's hangover from hell vanished into thin air. By the time the sun went down she was back to her usual self and if anything, more bright-eyed and bushy-tailed than she was before.

With Stelios's home having an entire guest wing, all six of us are in adjoining rooms, which are completely segregated from the rest of the building via a grand glass walkway. I was originally concerned that being holed up with Janie and Stelios might be a little too much for Oliver, but the guest wing is like a mansion in its own right. Consisting of six suites in total, each room is equipped with a self-contained high-spec kitchen, a hot tub and a bed fit for a king. Just a single one of these suites would blow most people's entire homes out of the water.

Hearing the shower come to a sudden stop, I turn my focus to my wild hair. The sun has never been friendly to my coarse curls and it seems the sunshine in Mykonos is no exception. My chocolate coils fall in a frazzled mess down my back, creating a crown of frizz around my face. Resorting to drowning my tresses in serum, I hope for the best with the help of a dozen bobby pins.

'You need to get dressed.' I say to Oliver, as he steps out of the glass booth. 'We need to leave in five minutes.'

Wrapping a towel around his waist, he pulls me towards him and I squeal as a drop of water falls from his hair and slips down my back.

'You've cheered up.' I remark, batting him away as he nuzzles his nose into my neck. 'Maybe we *should* get one of these showers at home.'

'Just because I don't like Stelios doesn't mean I don't like you...' He replies with a glint in his eye, softly pushing me towards the bed.

A delicious tingle runs along my spine as he kisses my neck, but before I can respond to his advances, a loud knocking disturbs us.

Untangling myself from a rather disappointed Oliver, I walk across the glistening tiles and fiddle with the handle to open the door.

'Hey!' Lianna grins, sashaying into the room in a fabulously sparkly dress. 'How do I look?'

'Amazing!' Waiting for Vernon to follow her inside, I allow the door to close behind them. 'That colour is great on you!'

'I know!' Heading straight for the mirror, Li twirls around and pouts as she poses for a selfie. 'Hurry up and get dressed. Stelios has arranged for us to have pre-dinner drinks on the terrace before we leave.'

Nodding in response, I shove my feet into my favourite pair of Suave stilettos and reach for my watch.

'Isn't this place incredible?' Vernon exclaims, wandering around the room and marvelling at the luxury fixtures and fittings. 'You have the shower thing as well, huh?'

'It's alright, I suppose.' Oliver takes a handful of clothes from the wardrobe and disappears into the bathroom.

Knowing his sudden change of attitude is due to our conversation about Stelios and Janie, I roll my eyes and fiddle with the buckle on my shoe.

'Oh, come on!' Vernon continues, as Oliver reappears dressed in a pair of chinos and a crisp shirt. 'This thing could all be yours one day.'

Discreetly kicking Lianna, I pluck a few dresses from the railing and hold them up for her opinion.

'Vern, I think Oliver's had enough of the Stelios jokes now.' Li warns, pointing to a grey floaty dress and dismissing the others. 'You've had your fun with the teasing.'

Giving him a knowing look, Lianna follows me into the bathroom as Oliver takes a couple of beers from the minibar.

'How's your room?' I ask, dropping my robe and shimmying into the dress.

'Pretty much identical to this one.' Perching on the edge of the bath, Lianna crosses her long legs and sighs as she looks around the enormous bathroom. 'I think I've fallen in love.'

'Fallen in love with what?'

'With everything!' Li explains, her eyes wide with lust as she admires the high-end toiletries. 'Stelios, this place, Mykonos in general...'

'That's a whole lot of love.' Motioning for her to zip me up, I remove a smudge of mascara from my cheek and quickly spritz myself in perfume.

'You are aware you've just made yourself dinner for the millions of mosquitoes out there, aren't you?' She mumbles, fiddling with the clasp on my dress. 'Gina's just done the same thing.'

'She's coming out tonight?' I ask in surprise. 'I expected her to have relapsed into her hangover.'

'Of course, she's coming!' Standing back to admire my dress, Lianna gives me the thumbs-up. 'Marc would rather chop off his legs than let her miss an opportunity like this.'

'Opportunity?' I repeat, leaning towards the mirror and dusting a fleck of dust from the skirt of my dress. 'It's just dinner, isn't it?'

'It's dinner with some of the most powerful men in Greece.' Li says dramatically, as she ushers me out of the bathroom. 'It's called *networking*.'

'I thought we were leaving *networking* at home.' Discovering Marc and Gina by the door with the guys, I break into a smile. 'When did you two get here?'

'Just now.' Marc replies, glancing down at his watch. 'We would have been here an hour ago if Gina didn't have to put her face paint on.'

Leading the way into the lobby, Marc turns the conversation to golf as the girls deliberately keep a few steps behind.

'Gina! You look incredible!' I gush, running my fingers over her hair and admiring her perfect makeup. 'I'm guessing Calix's hangover cure worked a treat?'

'It sure did!' Tugging on the hem of her short dress, Gina laughs happily. 'I don't know what was in there and I don't think I want to, but I feel like I've had ten hours sleep and a double espresso.'

'Well, whatever was in it, he should bottle the damn stuff and sell it.' Lianna replies, waiting for me to adjust the clasp on my shoe before continuing along the hallway. 'If it has this effect on everyone, he would make millions.'

In spite of consuming her weight in alcohol earlier, Gina looks better than I've seen her in a very long time. Her eyes are sparkling, her complexion is flawless and she's jollier than you would believe possible for someone who was blotto just a few hours ago. Her choice of clothing leaves little to be desired, but where Gina is concerned, that would be the case regardless of her alcohol consumption. The tiny slip dress she's wearing gives a whole new meaning to *little black dress.* It's a little too short, a little too tight and dare I say it, a little too nineties.

'What do you think of my dress?' Gina asks. 'Do you like it?'

'I love it!' Lianna answers quickly, looking both ways at the end of the lobby before deciding to turn right. 'Very retro!'

Deciding to keep my own opinions to myself, I agree with Li. 'If Cosmo is to be believed, retro is making a comeback.'

'This bad boy is twenty years old.' Gina cackles, adjusting her mammoth cleavage. 'It was my pulling dress back in the day!'

'Then why the hell are you wearing it now?' I ask, suddenly understanding why it's so ill-fitting.

'I stumbled across it when I was packing.' She explains breezily, smiling down at the ancient garment. 'I never imagined it would fit again, but once I realised it did, there was no way I was leaving it behind.'

Not wanting to be the one to tell her that just because it zips doesn't mean it fits, I smile sweetly as she continues to rave about her dress.

'This dress and I have had some great times together. She deserves one last hurrah before I pack her away for good.'

'You could send her to a charity shop.' I muse, tucking my clutch bag under my arm. 'Then someone else could show her a good time.'

'Maybe...' Gina purses her lips and sighs heavily. 'I just don't think I'm ready to say goodbye to her yet.'

'Say goodbye?' Lianna teases. 'It's just a bloody dress! Toss it into the recycling and move on.'

A look of hurt washes across Gina's face and I immediately feel bad for mocking her cherished dress.

'Leave her alone, Lianna.' I scold, following the sound of Vernon's laugh through a grand hallway. 'If Gina wants to relive her teenage years, just let her. Nineties dress or no nineties dress.'

'Actually, I think it's eighties.' Gina says seriously. 'I bought it from a flea market in my student days.'

'In that case, it's probably *fifties*.' Lianna whispers, shooting me a wink over her shoulder.

'What was that?' Gina asks, completely oblivious to Li's joke.

Spotting the guys up ahead, I swallow a giggle and link my arm through Gina's. 'Nothing. Just ignore her.'

Walking up the marble steps, I discover the guys are already chatting animatedly with a very proud-looking Stelios. Even Oliver has a silly grin on his face as Marc and Vernon pretend to practice golf swings. Pleased to see everyone seems to be getting along, I smile to myself and look around the stunning entertaining area. The sleek flooring is highlighted by a colossal chandelier that is hanging prestigiously in the centre of the room. An array of opulent sofas face towards the French windows, which have been pulled back to allow the ocean breeze to flow into the building.

'Canapé?' A handsome Greek butler asks, holding out a plate of alluring nibbles.

Still rather full due to the snacks we ate earlier, I open my mouth to decline, but the words don't quite come out as I anticipate.

'That would be lovely, thank you.' Plucking a blini from the platter, I grin happily and place it into a cloth napkin.

'It is my pleasure.' Moving on to Lianna, the polite butler nods and motions for us to sit down.

Taking a seat in a sumptuous armchair, I watch Stelios's employees straighten the many vases of flowers and wonder how Janie is able to relax with so many people milling around the place. It makes me a little uncomfortable when Summer comes over to collect Pumpkin for her walk. I just can't imagine wandering out of the shower to discover a chambermaid organising my underwear drawer.

The butler who served us our canapés approaches Stelios and subtly whispers in his ear, causing him to nod firmly and tap one of his many rings against the side of his glass.

'My friends!' Stelios says loudly, walking to the front of the room. 'We are now ready for our pre-dinner drinks. Please, come with me.'

Hiking up my dress, I slowly make my way up the steps and follow Stelios out onto the terrace, where Janie is sitting at the head of a long table. Automatically heading over to her, I pause when I spot a card bearing my name in front of a chair on my left.

'Why do we have designated seats?' I ask Janie, pulling out the chair and sitting down. 'I thought we were going out for dinner?'

'We are.' Janie replies casually, her Texan accent much softer than I remember it. 'But first, we have some drinks to enjoy here.'

Knowing how much Janie enjoys a good drink, or five, I smile in response and marvel at the beautiful calligraphy on the name cards. Considering we're only having a couple of drinks here, Stelios has really gone all out on the décor. Spectacular candelabras light up the dark sky, casting a flattering light over the pretty table and those gathered around it.

'Thank you so much for joining us...' Stelios begins, sounding like he's headlining a conference and not addressing friends in the comfort of his own home. 'In honour of your visit to my island, I have arranged for a very special drink for you all.'

Right on cue, a horde of eager butlers appear at the table and fill our glasses with golden bubbles.

Waiting until the staff have disappeared into the villa, Stelios holds his glass into the air.

'This Champagne is special. Very special. My friend in France sent this especially for you. For my family.'

My eyes flit to Janie and I try to ignore the feeling of unease in my stomach. At first, I thought Stelios's *family* comment was a slip of the tongue, but he must have addressed us as *his family* ten times already.

'Please, taste the Champagne.' He continues enthusiastically. 'I cannot wait a moment longer to hear what you think!'

Pulling my frosted flute towards me, I take a sip and look at the others for their reactions. Not being a wine connoisseur, I have no idea what I'm supposed to be tasting. Apart from it being fizzy, ice-cold and deliciously crisp, it tastes exactly the same as the cheap plonk we order at Artemis every Friday night.

'A complex bouquet with hints of straw and hay.' Vernon says casually, sticking his nose into the glass and sniffing loudly. 'Subtle notes of honey and peach, too.'

'Yes!' Visibly thrown by Vernon's take on the Champagne, Stelios clicks his fingers and his butlers reappear.

'Vernon and I used to own a bar in Barbados.' Lianna explains, beaming at Vernon proudly. 'Didn't we, Vern?'

'We sure did.' Raising the glass to his lips once more, Vernon nods appreciatively. 'And let me tell you, this is a very good bottle. The best.'

'It's the *very* best!' Stelios confirms, signals for his butlers to pour more Champagne. 'Only the best for my family.'

'I'd prefer a beer...' Oliver says cockily, much to my horror. 'No offence.'

Leaning over the table, Vernon tugs on Oliver's sleeve. 'Dude, this is around a hundred bucks a glass.'

'Just drink it, Oliver!' I hiss, completely mortified.

'It is no problem!' Stelios stammers, his cheeks flushing with embarrassment. 'No problem at all. Calix! *Calix!*'

Before I can reassure Stelios that Oliver *will* drink the excruciatingly expensive fizz, Calix returns with a silver tray bearing a single bottle of beer.

'Your beer, sir.' Handing over the bottle, Calix nods and disappears back into the villa.

When Calix said nothing was out of bounds in his job description he wasn't joking. First chauffeur and now butler. What's next? Window cleaner and masseur?

'Is this now to your satisfaction?' Stelios asks eagerly, waiting with bated breath while Oliver takes a swig.

Nodding in approval, Oliver gives Stelios a thin smile and I breathe a sigh of relief.

'Okay!' Stelios grins, swiftly shaking off the beer incident. 'Now that we all have a drink. I have a gift for you.'

Excited chit-chat echoes around the terrace and I look over at Janie for a clue as to what it could be.

'In front of you, you will find a box.' Stelios continues. 'Small box.'

Plucking a velvet presentation case from beside my name card, I glance around the table and notice everyone else has one, too.

'Please, look inside.' Standing next to Janie, Stelios animatedly motions for us to open our presents.

Carefully pulling on the gold ribbon, I hold the box under the candelabra and flip back the lid. A striking red stone glistens back at me, leaving me completely lost for words.

'What is it?' Gina whispers, holding her box up to the light.

'It is a ruby of the finest clarity.' Stelios explains with pride. 'My family, the Christopoulos family, has a medallion that signifies our unity.'

Reaching into his shirt, he pulls out a gold chain and produces the iconic medallion with glassy eyes.

'The ruby stone is the most important feature of the medallion and now I want to extend the honorary gem to all of you...'

Totally floored by the incredibly sentimental gift, I take the gleaming stone from its silk-lined box and turn it over in my hands as Stelios continues to preach about the meaning of family.

'My Janie has completed my circle.' He says seriously, his voice thick with emotion. 'My Janie is the final piece of my puzzle. My Janie's family, is *my* family...'

Chapter 8

Looking around the bustling bar, I attempt to block out the sound of Gina and Janie cackling like a pair of hyenas and absorb the buzzing atmosphere. It turns out the restaurant Stelios was so keen on taking us to was literally next door to his villa. The Haven, as it is so appropriately named, is tucked away on a quiet corner of the bay, shielded by a wall of grand palapas and flowing drapes. Impeccably dressed staff drift from table to table, ensuring nothing falls short of perfection for the many happy diners.

If we thought Azure was impressive, The Haven has raised the bar astronomically high. Think laidback Ibiza vibes seamlessly blended with quintessential Greek charm and you're halfway there. Glasses are being clinked together, smiles are escalating to laughter and the most delicious smells imaginable are drifting from the kitchen. A one-man band is singing on a driftwood platform, creating the ideal ambience to the picture-perfect setting.

Despite my reservations about networking with Stelios's contacts, each and every one of his associates was a pleasure to dine with. Their reserved nature meant that we barely knew they were there. The most I heard them speak was when they excused themselves to dash off to another meeting halfway through the meal. Not that anyone was fazed. Between listening to the live music and working our way through an incredible tasting menu, Stelios's associates were the last thing on our minds.

Resting my handbag on my lap, I discreetly slip my hand inside and hold the huge ruby in my palm. The heavy gem feels cold to touch as I run my fingers across the smooth surface. Stelios's excessive gifts seem a little forced and as much as I don't want to be ungrateful, I don't really know how I feel about them. I realise the guy is extremely wealthy, but to shower people you barely know with precious gemstones is extreme, to say the least.

Throughout the course of the meal, I've tried to convince myself this is just Stelios's way of welcoming us to his home and perhaps I am putting a little too much thought into it, but my gut is telling me something is off. I haven't managed to speak to any of the others about the grand gesture and being sandwiched between Oliver and Janie, I don't think I'm going to.

Surprisingly, Oliver didn't breathe a word about the medallion-inspired gift on the way over here, but I'm not sure whether his silence is a positive thing. Giving him a sideways glance, I watch him chatting with Marc and try to work out what he's thinking. With the wind in his hair and his eyes crinkled into a smile, you would never believe his nemesis is sitting just a few feet away. Although, to be fair, Stelios has no idea of the depths of Oliver's hatred for him. As far as he is concerned, Oliver is mildly irked at him for dating his mother. Stelios is completely oblivious to the fact Oliver would rather swim with alligators than give him his blessing to be with Janie.

'How was your meal?' Stelios asks, thanking the waiters as they subtly whip away our plates. 'All good? Yes?'

'It was beautiful.' Leaning to the left as my empty dessert bowl is removed, I smile gratefully. 'Everything was just perfect.'

'I couldn't fault a thing!' Gina adds, reaching for the drinks menu. 'The best meal I've had in ages.'

The rest of the group nod in agreement as Stelios looks on happily.

'Fantastic! I am very pleased to hear it!' Draping his arm around Janie's shoulder, he slips a wad of notes to one of the waitresses. 'The food here is the best in all of Mykonos.'

'It's certainly something special, that's for sure.' Vernon muses, yawning into the back of his hand. 'It reminds me a little of The Hangout.'

Suddenly seeing the resemblance to Li and Vernon's beloved Barbados bar, a lovely feeling washes over me as I remember the good times we shared there.

'I miss running a bar.' Looking around the restaurant wistfully, Lianna smiles and rests her elbows on the table. 'Don't get me wrong, I adore Suave, but nothing quite gets me going like the buzz of being the hostess. The energy of working with happy tourists and serving smiling faces for a living was so addictive. Do you know what I mean?'

'I know exactly!' Stelios replies, even though Lianna was clearly talking to Vernon. 'My first venture was a café, so I know. I know well.'

'You started in the hospitality industry?' Marc asks, sounding genuinely intrigued. 'How did you transition into the fashion world? What made you leave food and beverages behind?'

'There was no leaving behind.' Stelios coughs and leans forward in his seat, enjoying being the centre of attention. 'I own six restaurants and two hotels.'

I raise my eyebrows and pull my glass towards me, a little bemused by his revelation. Not only does Stelios own one of the biggest handbag businesses in the world, he also has six restaurants and a couple of hotels under his belt. Not to mention his bulging property portfolio and abundance of yachts.

'Ianthe takes my attention now, but my first love was hospitality.' He continues, his voice casual as he speaks. 'Working with people was what gave me life. Well, until I met my Janie. Now my Janie is what gives me life.'

Stelios stares lovingly at Janie and I kick Oliver beneath the table as he curses under his breath.

'We'll buy another bar one day.' Vernon says thoughtfully, as Lianna rests her head on his chest. 'We could even open a restaurant. I think we both know that's ultimately what we want...'

'If you want a restaurant, there is no better than this one.' Stelios says firmly, waving his arms around. 'This one... right here. The Haven. You should buy The Haven!'

Lianna and Vernon laugh gently and shake their heads.

'If only...' Li sighs. 'Our money is tied up in Suave right now and even if it wasn't, I'm going to guess this place is out of our price range.'

'But never say never.' Vernon adds, loosening the collar on his shirt. 'Who knows what the future holds?'

The table falls into a comfortable silence as a waiter hands around a selection of polished coffee menus. Running my eyes over the many options available, I finger the page before closing the cover and pushing it away.

'Then I buy it!' Stelios exclaims, causing me to physically jump in my seat. 'I buy The Haven for you, yes?'

A giggle travels around the group as we laugh at his joke. For someone who is a fierce businessman, Stelios Christopoulos is quite the comedian.

'Very funny...' Lianna replies, shuffling closer to Vernon as Marc snaps some photographs on his phone.

Signalling for us all to get in the frame, Marc stands up as Oliver and I wander over to where Gina and Janie are sitting. Positioning myself amongst my friends, I stick out my tongue and smile for the camera.

Too busy posing for pictures, I almost don't notice Stelios talking to a suited man in the shadows of the trees. Stern expressions are fixed on their faces as they quietly engage in an in-depth conversation.

'What's he doing?' Gina whispers to Janie, who looks just as clueless as the rest of us.

'Don't ask me!' Holding her hands in the air, Janie adjusts her zebra print dress and shakes her head. 'What that man does is his own business.'

Leaving the others to pose for pictures, I take a few steps back and shamefully try to eavesdrop on their conversation. Not being able to hear more than a few indecipherable murmurs, I turn my attention to Oliver and plant a soft kiss on his cheek.

'Are you good?' I ask, relieved to see he's still smiling, despite Stelios's many public displays of affection towards Janie. 'Did you enjoy your meal?'

'Yes and yes.' He replies, reaching across the table for his beer. 'Mykonos is pretty amazing.'

'I just knew you'd love it here!' Janie squeals, running over and throwing her arms around the pair of us. 'Hearing you say that makes me so happy!'

Hugging her back, I notice Oliver's eyes soften as we embrace one another warmly.

'You haven't seen anything yet!' Janie continues, happiness ringing through her voice as the others retreat to their seats. 'Stelios has so much more planned for you...'

'Cool...' Oliver smiles in response, but it doesn't quite meet his eyes.

Knowing we have three days to fill before the Ice Party, I'm intrigued to know what activities are on the agenda, but before I can ask, Stelios returns to the table.

'The deal is done!' He declares, looking extremely pleased with himself. 'The Haven, it is now yours.'

'I'm sorry?' I say in confusion, thinking I've misheard him. 'Could you repeat that?'

Looking around the table grinning inanely, Stelios points at Lianna and Vernon. 'The Haven is theirs.'

I stare at Stelios as I wait to hear the punchline, but something about his demeanour tells me he isn't joking.

'It's yours.' He repeats, his eyes sparkling as he studies their reaction. 'The Haven is my gift to you.'

Lianna opens and closes her mouth repeatedly, before finally regaining the use of her tongue.

'He's kidding, right?' She says to Janie, waiting for her to confirm that he is.

'No kidding!' Stelios laughs and holds his medallion to his lips. 'I do not kid! I buy for you.'

'Dude, you can't just *buy* someone a restaurant!' Vernon says in awe, shaking his head incredulously. 'That's insane.'

'Why not?' Stelios's face crumples as he tries to comprehend what all the fuss is about. 'You want, I buy.'

'Excuse me, I need to get some air.' Oliver says agitatedly, pushing out his chair and striding across the busy terrace with his drink in his hand.

Resisting the urge to go after him, I chew the inside of my cheek nervously and will the ground to swallow me up. If public displays of affection make me feel uncomfortable, public displays of extravagance make me even more so.

'As incredible as that offer is...' Lianna says carefully, pushing away her menu. 'We simply cannot let you buy us a restaurant, but I appreciate the gesture immensely.'

'You're unbelievably generous, Stelios.' Vernon stammers. 'Too generous, but she's right, we can't accept it.'

Seemingly lost for words, Stelios stares back at them blankly.

'Okay.' He says eventually, shrugging his shoulders and forcing a thin smile. 'It is no problem. No problem at all.'

Fidgeting with the clasp of my watch, I steal a glance over at Oliver and smile gratefully when Marc takes it upon himself to wander over to him.

'Maybe *we* should buy The Haven.' Draining her glass, Janie looks up at Stelios and bats her long eyelashes. 'You've been looking for a new investment.'

Nodding slowly, Stelios runs a hand through his black hair and purses his lips. 'Okay. We keep the restaurant.'

Clinking their glasses together, Janie and Stelios kiss briefly and toast their new venture, as though they've just purchased a pair of trainers and not a prestigious establishment.

Not quite believing what I've witnessed, I look down at the ruby in my handbag and try to process what the hell just happened here.

'It would appear we have some celebrating to do!' Gina babbles, reaching for her own drink and holding it in the air. 'To you guys!'

One at a time, we lift up our drinks and exchange bewildered looks as Stelios brushes off our stunned reactions.

'To you guys!' We all repeat in unison.

Raising my glass to my lips, I drain the contents and sit back as the others bombard Stelios with a million excited questions about his spontaneous purchase. While Stelios explains his decision to acquire The Haven, I turn my focus to Janie's delirious grin and wonder how she can possibly feel comfortable with such decadent purchases. With her coming from such a humble background, you'd think she would be a little more cautious.

I've always believed a fool and his money are easily parted, but when money is no object, do the same rules apply?

* * *

Strategically positioning myself beneath the air-conditioning, I bury my face in the pillow and allow my eyes to close. Despite Oliver being sprawled out next to me, he's at least six feet away and as a result, I can starfish like I'm the only girl in the world.

'It was so nice of Stelios to buy us such a lovely dinner.' I whisper, marvelling at how soft the sheets are. 'Wasn't it?'

'He didn't just buy dinner.' Oliver says scathingly, folding his arms behind his head. 'He bought the whole damn restaurant.'

'Wasn't that crazy?' I reply, intrigued to hear his opinion on the astonishing happenings at The Haven earlier.

'I can think of other words for it.' He scoffs. '*Crazy* isn't one of them.'

'He just *bought* it. Just like that.' I mumble to myself, staring up at the ceiling. 'Can you imagine if Li and Vernon would have accepted?'

'Most people would have. Luckily, they have more pride than to be bought like that.' Stuffing a pillow behind his head, he shuffles around on the bed to get comfortable. 'The guy thinks he can just throw his money around and people will come running.'

Nodding along, my mind drifts back to the precious gemstone in my handbag. 'The ruby thing was a little... *strange*. Don't you think?'

'Again, I can think of other words.' Oliver grumbles, pulling the blanket up to his chin.

'Do you think that's just what billionaires do when they have guests over?' I ask. 'Like how Eve buys fresh flowers and cupcakes when we go for dinner?'

'When I'm a billionaire, I'll let you know.'

Taking that as a *no,* I listen to the sound of the waves gently crashing against the shore on the beach down below.

'What did you do with your ruby?' I ask, suddenly realising I haven't seen him with it since we left the restaurant earlier.

Pointing to the bathroom, Oliver smiles wickedly and flicks off the bedside lamp. Following his gaze, I let out a gasp as I discover he's used the expensive jewel to prop open the bathroom door.

'*Oliver!*' I hiss, diving out of bed and grabbing the ruby from the tiled floor. 'You can't do that!'

'Why not?' He replies between yawns. 'The guy has doorstops made of gold in the main building.'

'I don't care if Stelios has unicorns holding the bloody doors open.' Frantically dusting down the gem on my pyjamas, I place it in the safety of my handbag along with mine. 'Don't be so ungrateful. Those rubies must have cost thousands.'

'It's not ungrateful to be freaked out by such a weird gesture.' Oliver retorts, rolling onto his side. 'And it's also not ungrateful to be freaked out by being referred to as *family* all the goddamn time.'

Not being able to argue with either of his very valid points, I decide to say nothing and slip under the sheets.

Kissing Oliver goodnight, I curl up into a ball and close my eyes once more. Maybe we're mistaking Stelios's kindness as being over the top and maybe that's simply because we just don't understand his lifestyle. After all, six rubies are a drop in the ocean for Stelios's finances. In the grand scheme of things, lavishing your partner's friends and family with outlandish gifts is hardly the worst crime in the world.

In fact, it's not a crime at all. Most people would be jumping for joy at Stelios's lavish presents, so why aren't I?

As I'm trying to persuade myself that Stelios's behaviour is normal for someone of his social stature, my eyelids become extremely heavy and I finally give in to the lure of some much-needed sleep. Overthinking innocent situations has always been my downfall, but the older I get, I still can't shake the habit.

My mother always warned me if you think too much, you'll create a problem that was never there in the first place and as the sound of the waves soothes me to sleep, I'm leaning towards her being right...

Chapter 9

Waking up in the villa feels incredibly surreal and waking up to two beaming butlers presenting us with breakfast is even more so...

Quickly grabbing the blanket to protect my modesty, my cheeks flush pink as the men bearing trays of croissants and coffees tactfully avert their eyes. Once confident I'm not going to subject them to an unfortunate nip slip, I thank them for the breakfast and smile gratefully as they nod and discreetly slip out of the bedroom.

'Well, that was rather strange.' I say to Oliver, whose hair is standing on end like a startled rabbit. 'Do you think Stelios wakes up like that every morning?'

'Definitely.' Yawning loudly, he takes a grape from the overflowing fruit bowl and throws back the sheets. 'He probably has someone to wipe his...'

'That's enough!' I interrupt, before the air turns blue. 'I get the picture, thank you very much.'

Managing a tiny smile, Oliver takes the silver trays and carries them out onto the balcony. Following the smell of freshly baked croissants, I stumble out of bed and trace Oliver's footsteps to the sprawling veranda, which is flooded with light from the morning sun. The inviting warmth hits me the second my feet hit the hot tiles and I allow myself a few moments to revel in the lovely sensation.

'Good morning!' A chirpy voice sings behind me. 'Sleep well?'

Forcing myself to spin around, I smile as I discover Lianna, Vernon, Marc and Gina on the adjacent balcony.

'Like a baby!' I reply, quickly grabbing my sunglasses from the dresser and hopping over the dividing wall. 'Did you?'

'Same.' Draping her legs over Vernon's lap, Lianna yawns and turns her face to the sun. 'If it wasn't for the heavies knocking on the door just now, I would have slept all day long.'

'It was certainly a shock, wasn't it?' I whisper, reaching for the coffee pot. 'But I don't think they'll come to our room again after I nearly flashed them.'

'They'll probably come twice...' Smothering her legs with tanning oil, Gina steals a strawberry from Marc's plate and chuckles.

The others join in with her laughter and I blow into my hot coffee, looking at her glistening legs dubiously.

'I have some sun lotion in our room. Do you want me to get it for you?' I offer, not wanting Gina to cook herself like a piece of streaky bacon.

'No, thank you.' Giving me a knowing look, Gina squirts more of the greasy oil into her hands. 'I'm perfectly fine with this.'

Remembering her warnings about mothering, I purse my lips and decide to keep shtum. If Gina wants to end this trip with a visit to a severe burns unit, that's her decision.

'Eat your breakfast.' Oliver instructs, pushing a plate of pastries towards me. 'It's going cold...'

Not needing to be told twice, I pick up my cutlery and look out at the incredible view. Being situated on a secluded corner of the island, Stelios's mansion is shielded by cliffs on either side, making you feel completely cocooned in its luxury. Janie must have to pinch herself waking up to this every day. The enormous villa, the dozens of staff and the impossible-to-ignore luxuries. I find it hard to accept that Stelios actually lives like this. For him, this isn't a treat, a special break or a glimpse into how the other half lives. It's simply his life.

'Stelios is really something, isn't he?' Vernon muses, pushing away his empty plate. 'What a character!'

Studying Vernon's face carefully, I try to decipher if he thinks Stelios being a *character* is a good personality trait or a glaringly obvious flaw.

'He's amazing!' Marc replies, a huge smile on his face as he reaches into his pocket and takes out his ruby. 'I mean, just look at this!'

I smile back at him, a little surprised by his glowing opinion of Stelios.

'Honestly, when I grow up, I want to be Stelios Christopoulos!' Marc continues, gaping at the gemstone as though it holds the answer to all of life's unanswered questions. 'The guy's a god!'

Nodding along, I finish my coffee and turn to Lianna and Gina. 'What do you guys think?'

'I think he's spectacular.' Lianna says adoringly, dropping her sunglasses onto the table. 'He's the most generous man I've ever met.'

Vernon coughs playfully and raises his eyebrows.

'Apart from you, of course.' She adds, reaching up and kissing his cheek. 'Stelios's only fault is that he's *too* generous.'

'I agree.' Vernon adds. 'He should be careful, or people could take advantage.'

Gina nods in agreement and I let my friend's opinions of Stelios sink in. Whereas Oliver and I have been questioning Stelios's extravagant actions, it seems the rest of the gang have a different view of him entirely.

'Have you got your golf shoes ready?' Marc asks Oliver, who is devouring his croissants in complete silence.

'Golf shoes?' Oliver repeats, shielding his eyes from the sun. 'What are you talking about?'

'You didn't get the letter?' Reaching below the table, Marc retrieves a piece of paper and hands it to Oliver. 'This was on our breakfast tray. Stelios has arranged a golf trip.'

Reading the letter over his shoulder, I feel my skin prickle with excitement as I take in the words on the pages. It appears that while the boys whack a ball around acres of land, us girls are going to be treated to our own day of fun, Janie style. Usually, the idea of a liquid lunch with my mother-in-law is enough to send me running for the hills, but today I am hugely grateful.

Ever since we arrived here in Mykonos, I've been itching for some time with Janie away from Stelios and Oliver. I want to ask about her life here with Stelios and not hear the edited version she tells when he is sitting by her side. I want to hear the cold, hard truth, no holds barred. The same dirty laugh floats out of her mouth, the same overdone makeup is plastered on her face and the same hideous dress sense is in full swing, but something about Janie has changed and I can't quite put my finger on what it is. Today will give me an opportunity to discover exactly what's going on with her and Stelios and a chance to establish where this relationship of theirs is going.

'You *love* golf!' I say to Oliver, rubbing his arm encouragingly.

He responds with a look that says *I do love golf, but I hate Stelios* and I bite my lip.

'Why the glum face?' Gina teases, positioning her chair to face the sun. 'This will give you some time to bond with your new stepdad.'

'Or to hit him with a club...' Oliver grumbles, tossing a grape at Gina.

'Oh, come on!' Marc protests, taking Oliver's cap and dropping it onto his head. 'Who here would want Stelios as an in-law?'

Right on cue, everyone raises their hands and I suddenly feel guilty for questioning Stelios's intentions. Taking a final look at the jaw-dropping landscape, I hold up my hand and shrug my shoulders apologetically at Oliver.

'With views like that, who could possibly say no?'

*   *   *

'Is this another one of your throwbacks?' I ask Gina, who is admiring her garish jumpsuit proudly. 'I haven't seen one of those in decades!'

'It is indeed!' She replies, shaking her legs to show off the baggy trousers in all their glory. 'How can you tell?'

Not wanting to admit the hideous outfit just screams MC Hammer and bad fancy-dress costumes, I rack my brains for a suitable adjective to describe the monstrous ensemble.

'It's quite obviously vintage.' Lianna says quickly, coming to my rescue. 'They just don't make clothes the same these days.'

Flashing me a discreet wink, Lianna tosses her magazine onto the coffee table as Janie steps into view.

'Finally!' Gina yells, standing up as Janie sashays along the hallway. 'What time do you call this?'

Laughing off Gina's remarks, Janie envelopes the three of us in a huge bear hug.

'It's called being fashionably late!' She cackles, giving Gina's jumpsuit a strange look. '*Fashionably* being the operative word.'

I look down at Janie's orange minidress and resist the urge to tell her that people in glass houses shouldn't throw stones.

'So, what's on the agenda?' Lianna asks, dusting herself down. 'I can't wait to explore Mykonos!'

'In that case, let's get going!' Adjusting her floppy hat, Janie turns on her heel. 'But first...'

Wandering over to the bar, she takes four tiny glasses and places them in a row on the counter. Before she can make another move, two members of staff run across the foyer and take over. Wearing slick suits, they mumble a few words to Janie in Greek, which she strangely seems to understand and fill the glasses with a clear spirit.

'This is how we start the day here at *Casa Janie!*' She declares, gesturing for us to help ourselves to a glass. 'It'll put hairs on your chest, that's for sure!'

Choosing not to tell her that hairs on my chest are the last thing I want, I hesitantly take a glass and hold it to my lips.

'What is it?' I ask, grimacing as a strong smell of aniseed assaults my nose.

'It's ouzo!' Janie says proudly. 'Stelios's favourite! Go ahead, taste it.'

Peeking into the shot glass, I feel my stomach churn and shudder. After devouring a huge breakfast of exotic fruits, rich pastries and a variety of meats, I don't think adding high-strength alcohol to the mix is a very good idea. Clearly not having the same concerns, Gina clinks her glass against Janie's and throws it back in one swift gulp.

Knowing Janie isn't going to let me leave without drinking the ouzo, I take a deep breath before copying Gina. My face immediately screws up as the ouzo slips down my windpipe and crashes into my stomach like a firework.

'Who wants another?' Janie cheers, not waiting for a response before beckoning her butlers to line them up.

'Not for me.' Wiping her tongue on a paper napkin, Lianna shakes her head.

'Me neither.' I splutter, dashing to the bar in search of some water. 'One is quite enough, thank you very much.'

Accepting a bottle from one of the men, I whip off the cap and down half the contents.

'I'll have another!' Gina says, hooting loudly as she and Janie dance around the bar. 'I might even have two!'

Watching the pair of them giggle like teenagers, I am reminded of Gina's pledge to steer clear of alcohol for the rest of the trip.

'Do you think that's wise?' I ask, wondering if I can find Calix and order his hangover remedy in advance. 'Remember what happened yesterday?'

'Nope, I don't remember a thing about yesterday and I would like to keep it that way.' Gina retorts cockily, already going in for another shot of ouzo.

Raising my eyebrows at Lianna as Janie motions for us to follow her to the door, I try to waft the stench of ouzo out of my hair. No matter how far away from the bar we walk, the medicinal smell creeps after us in full force, refusing to be left behind.

Coming to a stop in the entrance hall, Janie waits patiently as two guards step out of the shadows and lead the way outside.

'How the hell do you get used to this?' I murmur to Janie, who casually walks outside as though dumb and dumber aren't stalking us like prey. 'They give me the creeps!'

'Who? Ioannis and Georgios?' She hoots, pointing to the two massive minders. 'They're a pair of teddy bears. Aren't you, boys?'

Ioannis and Georgios offer her a subtle nod in response and inspect the limo before signalling for us to get inside. Giving them a dubious glimpse, I wave at Calix as he appears from the villa and jumps into the driver's seat.

My warm skin sticks to the leather as I slide closer to Janie and rearrange my dress.

'Is that... is that a tattoo?' I gasp, pointing at Janie's ankle in shock as a flash of black catches my eye. 'It is! Isn't it?'

Smiling at her ankle with sheer admiration, Janie places her tanned leg across my knee. At first, the small inking just above her foot resembles a messy scribble, but on closer inspection, I see it is some kind of stick symbol.

'Do you like it?' She asks, twisting her leg from side to side.

Dreading to think what Oliver is going to say about his mother having acquired a tattoo, I think hard for a suitable reply.

'I love it!' Lianna exclaims, once again saving me from an incredibly awkward moment. 'What does it mean?'

'It's a Greek symbol.' Janie begins, smiling at the tattoo. 'It says... well, it doesn't matter what it says. It was a gift from Stelios.'

Squinting at the inking once more, I try to work out what it could possibly say. From my angle, it almost looks like a half-finished game of hangman.

'We should all get tattoos!' Gina cries suddenly, jumping up and down in her seat. 'On my Ibiza trip...'

'1999, by any chance?' Lianna asks sarcastically.

'That's the one!' Gina replies, not realising that Li is poking fun. 'My friends at the time, they all got matching tattoos and I've always regretted not joining in.'

'You've always regretted not getting a booze-fuelled tattoo as a teenager?' I say dismissively, not quite believing what I'm hearing. 'You've got to be kidding me?'

'It's not about the tattoo itself.' Gina explains. 'It's about what the tattoo represented.'

'And what did it represent?' Not having an ounce of faith in a drunken holiday tattoo being a good idea, I shake my head. 'Come on, enlighten me.'

'It represented freedom, youth and vitality.' Inhaling deeply, Gina closes her eyes and smiles to herself. 'It represented faith, hope and liberty.'

'You got all that from a damn tattoo?' Janie jokes, pushing Gina's arm playfully.

'I got all that and more...' Opening her eyes, Gina looks down at Janie's tattoo. 'That's it, I'm getting a tattoo. Who's with me?'

'I'll get a tattoo with you.' Lianna fires back, not hesitating for a millisecond. 'Why the hell not?'

Shooting her a glare, I wonder what has got into my friends. Is there something in the water here in Mykonos that sends people on a bungee jump to insanity?

'Oh, to hell with it! Count me in.' Shrugging her shoulders, Janie gives Gina a high-five. 'I've already got one. What's one more?'

Feeling my jaw drop open, I stare at them in disbelief as Janie raps on the privacy screen to get Calix's attention.

'Calix, can you take us to the tattoo studio?' She asks, as Gina shrieks with glee.

Holding my head in my hands, I screw up my nose and groan. Little over an hour ago, I was blissfully enjoying my breakfast under the morning sun. Now, I am being whisked to a tattoo parlour against my will. How? How did this happen?

'You're not seriously going to do this, are you?' I ask, becoming increasingly perturbed by the drastic change of plan. 'I thought we were exploring Mykonos.'

'We *are* exploring Mykonos!' Janie protests, steadying herself on the seat next to her as Calix swings around a corner. 'I'm taking you to Mykonos's best tattoo studio! What better way to discover the island?'

Knowing that the harder I push against this the more they will fight for it, I try a different tactic.

'Don't you think you should run the idea past Marc first?' I say lightly, trying my hardest to act like I no longer care what they do. 'I'm sure he would be very interested in what you are about to do.'

'What I choose to do with my body is no one else's business.' Gina says firmly, obviously taking her impulsive idea super seriously. 'I may be a wife and a mother of three, but right now, I am Gina Cockburn and I am going to bloody well enjoy it!'

Holding my hands up to surrender, I turn to watching the world rush past the window as the others chat about their spontaneous detour. I had such high hopes for today. I was really looking forward to reconnecting with my mother-in-law, but instead, I am rushing across the island in a last-minute dash for Gina to live out her teen fantasies and unbelievably, Janie and Li are getting in on the action, too.

'We're here!' Janie sings, reaching for her handbag as Calix brings the limousine to a stop by the side of the road.

Not waiting for the engine to be turned off, Gina pulls on the handle and jumps out onto the hot pavement.

'*No! Wait!*' Janie shouts after her, making a grab for Gina's jumpsuit and missing.

Shouting in Greek, Ioannis and Georgios leap out of the limo at lightning speed and hustle Gina back into the vehicle.

'What the…' Gina curses, as Mr and Mr Scary patrol the perimeters of the vehicle.

'You get used to it.' Waiting for the signal from Ioannis before accepting his hand and stepping out of the limo, Janie slips on her oversized sunglasses.

'Does that happen every time you go out?' I ask, smiling at a few passers-by as they stop to admire the limousine. 'It seems a bit dramatic.'

Janie nods as Georgios holds open the door to the tattoo studio and I apprehensively follow her inside.

'It comes with the territory...'

Grimacing in response, I look around the studio nervously as Gina and Li make a beeline for the portfolios.

'What can I do for you?' A heavily tattooed man behind the counter asks.

As they excitedly inform him that they want matching tattoos to mark their trip to Greece, I walk around the room and study the various images on the walls. A collection of intricate sketches is displayed for customers to see. Some beautiful, some not so beautiful, but each and every one is distinctively individual.

Frowning at a scary-looking skull design, which has a knife protruding through one of the eye sockets, I spin around when I hear Gina mention a full sleeve.

'You don't think it would be a little too much?' Lianna asks, looking down at her arm and then back to the page.

'A little?' I hiss, practically falling over with shock. 'Are you two drunk?'

'What do you think?' Li says to Janie, as though I'm not even in the room. 'Should we just go for it?'

Pursing her lips as she looks at the intense design, Janie nods and points to another sketch. 'Maybe we could just get half a sleeve...'

'Alright!' I yell, positioning myself between the tattoo artist and Gina. 'That's quite enough! This is getting out of hand.'

'We also have a whole bunch of colour tattoos.' The tattoo artist says regardless, passing another folder over my head to Lianna.

Keeping my gaze fixed on Gina, who appears to be the ringleader in this charade, I narrow my eyes to show how serious I am.

'Gina, I'm not going to stand by and watch you cover your entire arm in a tattoo that you have put absolutely no thought into.' I warn sternly, lowering my voice to a whisper as to not offend the bulky tattoo artist. 'Getting a tiny tribute inking is one thing, but *this* is quite another.'

Almost unbelievably, Gina quickly gives in and flips back to the small designs.

'I say we go for this.' She says decidedly, pushing the folder towards the tattoo artist and pointing to a small sketch of a plane. 'What do you guys think?'

Taking a closer look, I squint as I try to decipher the Greek writing next to the wing.

'I like it!' Janie says, running her fingers over the paper.

'Me too!' Digging her purse out of her handbag, Li hands a wad of notes to the tattoo artist. 'Let's do it!'

'Wait a minute!' I yell, as they start to walk into the workshop. 'Just hold fire. What does that say?'

Holding out his hand for the folder, the tattoo artist shrugs his shoulders and scratches his beard.

'No regrets.' He says uncertainly, after studying the design for a moment too long. 'It says *no regrets*.'

Not being satisfied with his blasé response, I shake my head as the others smile back at him.

'Perfect! I couldn't have picked anything better myself!' Gina cries, practically dragging him to the chair. 'Come on! What are we waiting for?'

Not wanting to say how completely ironic that is, I slowly walk behind them and take a seat on a battered old bench. My skin prickles uncomfortably as within seconds they all have stencils printed onto their wrists. Scrambled chatter fills the room as they grab their phones and take adrenaline-fuelled selfies to mark the occasion. Choosing to abstain from the jovialities, I look at the clock on the wall and wonder what the hell I am doing here.

'Do *you* think this is a good idea?' I whisper to Ioannis, who is staring straight ahead blankly. 'Yes? No?'

Without flinching, he briefly glances down at me before returning his gaze back to Janie. Taking that as a *no,* I tap my foot impatiently as the tattoo artist taps a tired leather lounger and gestures for someone to get on.

'Who's going first?' He asks, pulling on some latex gloves and fiddling with a frankly frightening vibrating tool.

'You should go first, Gina.' Lianna mumbles quietly, looking nervous for the first time in this whole process. 'After all, this *was* your idea.'

Without a hint of doubt, Gina squeals with excitement and immediately hops onto the chair.

Hearing the infamous buzz of the needle, I look away and pretend to be engrossed in my manicure. Gina's shrieks surround me as my gaze drifts to a design on the wall which bears the words *act in haste, repent at leisure*. Smiling to myself, I watch Lianna

and Janie wait in line for their turn and resist the urge
to tell them to have that tattooed instead...

Chapter 10

'I still can't believe you went through with it.' I mutter to Janie, who is sprawled out on the lounger next to me as gentle waves rush up the sand to greet us. 'I really can't.'

'It's not a big deal.' Glancing down at the newly acquired inking, Janie sighs and reaches for her drink. 'It's only a drawing...'

'A *permanent* drawing.' I correct, glad to not be confined to the shade like the rest of them.

Removing her hat, Janie allows her hair to fall around her shoulders. 'Clara, nothing in this life is permanent.'

'I can assure you, that thing isn't going anywhere.' I retort, picking up a handful of sand and admiring how soft it is.

'Even so, at one point, it was exactly what I wanted...'

Peering at her over the rim of my sunglasses, I try to work out why Janie seems so different. She looks the same, she sounds the same, but Janie's certainly changed, that's for sure. She's softer, somehow. I've tried to brush it off, but Janie is most definitely a shadow of the woman she used to be.

Noticing Gina and Lianna are dozing under the palm trees to our left, I take the opportunity of being alone to delve into the mystery of Janie's life here.

'How are you finding life in Mykonos?' I ask casually, rolling onto my side to face her. 'How does Greece compare to London, or Texas, for that matter?'

Pointing at the glistening water in front of her, Janie smiles brightly. 'There's no comparison. Things are just... *easier* here.'

'Easier?' I repeat, taking a sip of my pína colada. 'Are you talking about the money?'

'I'm not going to lie to you, the money helps, but it's not only that.' Reaching for her own drink, she plucks her glass from its resting place in the sand. 'I don't have to pretend here. Mykonos has given me a chance to wipe the slate clean and start again. I can be *me* here and drop the mask. I can knock down the walls I've hidden behind for so long. Finally!'

'That's so lovely to hear. I'm really happy for you.' Resting my chin in my hand, I study her face closely, trying to read between the lines. 'So, this life here with Stelios, is it the real deal? Is this where you see your future?'

'Of course, it is.' Staring back at me blankly, Janie attempts to pull her frozen brow into a frown. 'Why would you ask that?'

'No reason.' I stammer, hoping I haven't caused offence. 'It's just a lot to take in, that's all. The bodyguards, the villa, the lavish lifestyle. It just seems so... *temporary.*'

'Temporary?' She repeats, a tone to her voice indicating I've hit a nerve. 'Tell me, Clara, what would be *temporary* about it?'

Desperately searching for a way to explain my point without adding to her outrage, I stir my straw around my glass.

'Please don't take this the wrong way.' I begin, pushing myself into a sitting position. 'It's just... it's just I find it hard to believe *this* is where your future lies. I'm overjoyed you're happy. I really, really am. To see this other side of you is amazing, but no one really lives like this. The bubble Stelios lives in isn't real life.'

Janie simply responds with a slight nod of the head, so I carry on regardless.

'I'm not against you having some fun out here with Stelios. Who *wouldn't* want to live like this for a little while?' I attempt a small laugh and stop when Janie doesn't join in. 'I'm just concerned because you seem different here. It's like you're still Janie, but somehow, you're not. My worry is that you're changing yourself to fit in with Stelios and his lifestyle.' Shuffling closer to her, I place my hand on her arm. 'Don't lose who you *are* in your bid to get what you *want*.'

Staring back at me with an expression I can't quite read, Janie eventually smiles and takes off her sunglasses.

'I appreciate your concern, Clara, but you don't need to be worried about any of those things.' Looking over her shoulder as Lianna stirs in her sleep, she drops her voice to a whisper. 'Being over here *has* changed me. It has changed me in ways I never imagined possible and I couldn't be more grateful for it.'

Waiting for her to explain, I tuck my hair behind my ears to prevent it from blowing into my face.

'Mykonos is my future just as much as Stelios is my future.' Her eyes appear glassy and she slips on her sunglasses to hide it. 'But neither Mykonos or Stelios are the reasons for me changing. They have simply allowed me to remove the armour I've kept up for so long. The Janie you knew was a reflection of how the world treated me, but I'm still here. I'm just... *happy*.'

A lump forms in my throat and I suddenly hate myself for questioning Janie's motives in being here.

'The only thing that isn't real about my life here, is that you guys aren't in it.' Janie says sadly. 'Having Oliver's blessing would be the cherry on the cake. Once I have that, I can finally accept this is my destiny.'

For the first time, I recognise how hard it must be for Janie to be here with her son refusing to be a part of it.

'Oliver *will* come around to Stelios' I reply, not believing this myself. 'He just needs a little more time.'

'I very much doubt it. I know my son and I know when his mind is made up, it's made up.' Janie looks down at the tattoo on her ankle and exhales heavily. 'I wish things were different, but I can't force Oliver to accept Stelios. He's a grown man and he makes his own decisions...'

Looking down at the ground, I drag my toes through the sand and try to think of something to say to raise the mood. A loving relationship is exactly what we've all wanted for Janie. She's been crying out for someone to spend her life with for so long. It's completely unfair of Oliver to throw shade over it now that she has finally found happiness.

'Leave Oliver to me.' I say determinedly, taking Janie's hand in mine and squeezing it firmly. 'If I can make him trade his morning bacon sandwiches for kale smoothies, this should be a piece of cake...'

*   *   *

Thanking Calix for driving us back to the villa, I dust a few grains of sand from my dress before heading up the steps and into the cool building. After our lazy afternoon on the beach, Janie took us for a bite to eat at a cute bakery in a neighbouring village. With our stomachs filled with vanilla cupcakes and refreshing lemonade, we jumped back into the limo and made the short journey home, high on sunshine and sugar.

I did worry the girls would be full of regret after our impulsive trip to the tattoo parlour this morning, but even as we collapse onto the couches in the sitting room they're *still* raving about their new inkings.

'Well, what do you think?' Gina asks Calix, waving her scrawled-on wrist in his face. 'Do you like it?'

Narrowing his eyes, Calix's cheeks flush and he covers his mouth awkwardly.

'It's… nice.' He stutters, tripping over his tongue in his attempt to spit his words out. 'Very… yes… very nice.'

Shooting him a questioning look, I frown as he quickly excuses himself and leaves the room in a fit of hysterics. His muffled laughter echoes around the hall, but before I can chase after him to query his reaction to Gina's tattoo, Stelios and the guys return home.

'My Janie!' Stelios exclaims, running through the foyer and enveloping Janie in a warm embrace. 'How I have missed you, my Janie!'

Watching them chat affectionately about their day apart, I look up as Vernon collapses onto the couch next to us.

'What did you girls get up to today?' He asks, smiling at the sight of Janie and Stelios cuddling on the opposite sofa. 'Anything fun?'

Exchanging excited glances, Lianna and Gina hold out their wrists and smile broadly. Not being too sure how Vernon is going to react to discovering his wife has gained a Kavos-style inking in his absence, I hold my breath as he squints at their arms.

'You got tattoos?' Vernon cries. 'That's so cool! I like it!'

'You do?' Grinning widely as he takes her arm for a closer look, Lianna squeals with relief.

'*You do?*' The words slip out of my mouth before I can stop them and Gina shoots me a deathly stare.

'Yeah.' Vernon says cheerily. 'Identical tattoos, you're like sorority sisters.'

'I have one, too!' Janie yells, wriggling out of Stelios's grip and waving her own arm in the air. 'Does that mean I'm in the sorority?'

'What's going on in here?' Marc asks, kicking off his shoes as he and Oliver finally join us.

'We got matching tattoos!' Gina announces, like she's just found the winning lottery ticket.

Recognising the look of alarm on Oliver's face, I hold my hands up in defence. 'Not me. I was just an innocent bystander.'

Shaking his head to indicate he doesn't want to get involved, Oliver kisses my cheek and excuses himself to get a shower.

'I don't know about you guys, but we have had an *amazing* day!' Marc gushes, walking across the room to Stelios and holding out his hand. 'Thank you! Thank you so much.'

Seemingly oblivious to the fact his wife has gained a permanent sketch in his absence, Marc continues to wax lyrical about his incredible day at the golf course.

Not wanting to be subjected to boy talk, I leave the others to chat amongst themselves and slip away in search of my husband. After a few wrong turns, I eventually locate the guest wing and knock lightly on our door before letting myself in.

'Hey!' Flashing Oliver a grin, I throw myself down onto the bed next to him. 'I thought you were having a shower?'

'I'm just taking five minutes out first.' He yawns, tugging his sweaty t-shirt over his head and tossing it onto the floor.

'If I were you, I wouldn't leave it any longer.' I say teasingly, wafting a hand under my nose. 'I could smell you out in the hall.'

Playfully batting me with a pillow, Oliver laughs and gently pulls me towards him.

'How was golf?' I ask, hoping to hear he's bonded with Stelios over a love of chequered shirts and small balls. 'Judging by the way Marc is talking out there, I'm guessing you all had a lot of fun.'

'You can hardly call it *golf* when you're followed by security the whole damn time and driven around like an old lady at a Florida retirement park.' He sneers, rolling his eyes.

'Marc certainly seems to have enjoyed himself...'

'Well, Marc would, wouldn't he? He spent the entire time schmoozing Stelios's business associates. He was like a pig in...'

Covering his mouth with my hand, I finish his sentence by planting a kiss on his nose.

'What about you?' He asks, stretching his arms above his head. 'Good day?'

'*Interesting* day...' I reply, recalling tattoo-gate. 'Didn't you see the tattoos in there?'

'Yeah.' Walking over to the minibar, Oliver grabs a couple of bottles of water and throws one to me. 'What the hell was that about?'

'It was the weirdest thing.' Taking a gulp from the cold bottle, I sit in a cross-legged position and shake my head. 'It all started when we were in the limo and I spotted Janie's new tattoo...'

'My *mom* has a *tattoo*?' He growls, wiping his mouth on the back of his hand.

'Yes.' Not wanting to make a big deal out of it, I attempt to swiftly move on. 'When Gina saw it, she decided she also wanted a tattoo. After that, it just started to snowball. Lianna wanted one and before I knew what was happening, your mum was having another as well!'

'She has *two* tattoos?' Oliver shrieks, leaning against the wall in shock. 'This is all Stelios's doing! He's supposed to be looking after her over here! Not encouraging her to mutilate her body like this!'

'The tattoos aren't down to Stelios!' I reply, deciding to leave out the part about Stelios's gift of an inking. 'And he *is* looking after her. *No one* can tame your mother, Oliver, let alone talk her out of doing something she wants to do.'

'I'm not going to argue with you...' Stepping out of his shorts, he mumbles something I don't quite catch before rubbing his face agitatedly. 'Let's just agree to disagree.'

Recognising that now isn't the time to work on project *Make Oliver Stelios's New Best Friend*, I kick off my sandals and divert the conversation to Gina.

'Anyway...' I sing, tugging on his arm. 'I think Gina is on the verge of having some sort of midlife crisis.'

'She's not having a midlife crisis.' Oliver says in Gina's defence. 'A stupid tattoo is a stupid tattoo, but it's not enough to equal midlife crisis.'

'It's not just the tattoo. She's constantly reminiscing about her teenage years, she's wearing her old *pulling outfits* from two decades ago...' Reeling off the many things Gina has done these past couple of days that prove my point, I follow Oliver out onto the balcony. 'Not to mention how much she's been drinking lately. The tattoo is just the tip of a very big iceberg.'

'She's just blowing off some steam. Don't read too much into it.' Collapsing onto a lounger in his boxer shorts, Oliver picks up my magazine from the floor. 'You should direct your concern towards my mom. I know I am.'

Gingerly sitting down on the sunbed next to him, I watch a tiny bird as it hops along the railing in front of me.

'I know you don't want to hear this, Oliver, but your mum is happy here with Stelios. She's happy and she's settled. This is her life now. She isn't going to get bored and come running back to England with her tail between her legs.' Pausing for effect, I lick my dry lips. 'She's finally found where she wants to be. The only thing standing in her way, is you.'

Keeping a stony expression on his face, Oliver looks out to sea and remains completely silent.

'Your refusal to accept Stelios is the only blemish on her horizon.' Twisting my wedding ring around my finger, I prod him with my foot and smile softly. 'If you want your mum to be happy, *truly* happy, you know what you have to do...'

Chapter 11

'Can you see it, Mummy?' Noah asks, holding an odd-looking rock towards the camera and pointing at a tiny swirl. 'It's a *dinosaur!*'

'Wow!' Bringing the phone closer to my face, I frown at the image on the screen. 'That's a huge… *dinosaur*, Noah! Where did you find him?'

'Mummy, it's a *girl* dinosaur!' Noah giggles, placing the stone even closer to the camera lens. 'Look!'

'Of course, it's a girl dinosaur!' Forcing myself to laugh, I shake my head. 'Silly me!'

As Noah continues to show me various different stones and *dinosaurs*, I nod along from my position on the balcony. It seems two days without his parents haven't affected Noah in the slightest. If anything, he seems happier than ever. Sitting on my father's knee, Noah has been chatting animatedly for the past thirty minutes. Too absorbed in his storytelling, he's completely oblivious to my mum hovering in the background for some screen time.

Making all the right noises as Noah shows off Pumpkin's security guard outfit, I lean over the balustrade and look down at the beach. Stelios, Marc, Vernon and Oliver are playing cards under an enormous canopy. Their boisterous laughter drifts across the sand as Marc slams his cards down on the table and cheers loudly. Pleased to see Oliver is joining in with the fun and games, I return my attention to the video call.

'We're going to a hamster race tomorrow!' Noah says cheerily. 'Can we get a hamster when you get back?'

'Erm, I'll have to run that past your dad, but leave it with me.' Realising my battery is about to die, I head back inside and take a seat at the dressing table. 'Can you please put Grandma on for a moment, Noah?'

Nodding at the screen, Noah jumps off my dad's knee and hands the phone to my mum.

'Bonjour!' She trills, holding the screen too close to her face.

'Mum, we're in Greece, not France!' Laughing at her stumped reaction, I shake my head and search the drawers for my charger.

'What's Greek for *hello?*' She asks, screwing up her nose. 'Is it *ola?* Or is that Spanish? You know, I should know this with all the Greek food we eat down at...'

'Never mind that. How's Noah been?' I interrupt, finally locating the charger beneath a pile of bikinis. 'And Pumpkin, how is she?'

'Fine! They're both doing absolutely fine!' My mum replies, attempting to turn the camera around and succeeding only in showing me the ceiling. 'Look at them. Happy as can be!'

'Mum... Mum, that's the ceiling!' I grumble, feeling a headache coming on.

'There's Pumpkin!' Wiggling the camera around and making me feel nauseous in the process, she whistles to get Pumpkin's attention. 'Say *hello* to your mum, Pumpkin!'

The screen jumps to her feet and I roll my eyes. 'I can't see anything other than your slippers.'

'Look at her face!' She continues regardless. 'I think she's even happier here than she is at home! Aren't you Pumpkin? Yes, you are! Yes, you are!'

Hearing more laughter float into the room from the beach, I decide to wrap up the call.

'Well, I'm glad to hear everything is going well. I was worried Noah might be feeling a little homesick.'

'Not at all!' My mum babbles, finally learning how to flip the camera around. 'We're all fine here. You go and enjoy your holiday!'

Smiling back at her, I wave at the screen and hover my finger over the *end call* button.

'Oh, wait!' She cries suddenly. 'Is Janie there? It's been a while since we have DVD called!'

Knowing very well that once my mother and Janie get talking they won't stop until the sun goes down, I shake my head regretfully. 'It's a *video call*, Mum and no, she's not here. Sorry.'

'Oh, that's a shame...' She says sadly, resting a hand on her hip as my dad yells in the distance. 'One moment, Clara, your father is talking to me... *What's that Henry? Aunt Lucinda is here?*'

Aunt Lucinda. The woman who smokes a hundred cigarettes a day and talks to anyone who will listen about her ingrowing toenail is the last thing I need right now.

'Clara, do you want to talk to...'

My pulse races as my mum rushes to the front door with the phone firmly in her hand.

'The signal's going, Mum. Sorry, Mum! The signal, it's...' Jabbing at the *end call* button, I breathe a sigh of relief at avoiding the dreaded Aunt Lucinda and drop the phone onto the dressing table.

Not wanting to risk her calling back, I turn off the handset and grab my flip-flops from the side of the bed. Catching a glimpse of myself in the mirror, I pause to twist my hair into a ponytail before heading for the door. The beautiful aroma of Stelios's home envelopes me as I make my way through the villa. Think subtle lily and sweet peony, with a hint of amber and soft spice. It almost puts you into a dreamlike state as it carries you through the building, refusing to let go without leaving its footprint on you. The delicious scent is still with me as I reach the beach a few minutes later.

Kicking off my flip-flops, I swoon as silky-soft sand slips between my toes like talcum powder.

'Where's Stelios?' I ask, suddenly realising he is no longer here.

'He's gone to collect my winnings!' Marc stammers, a look of sheer disbelief etched on his face.

'I hope you've been playing nicely.' Knowing that Marc is the Poker King, it doesn't surprise me one bit that he's cleared the others out. 'What were you guys playing for?'

'A freaking limo!' Vernon hoots, grabbing a card as the wind tries to whisk it away.

'A limo?' I repeat sceptically. 'What the hell are you talking about?'

'Stelios doesn't play for money.' Bending the peak on his cap, Oliver raises his eyebrows. 'He plays for limousines, apparently.'

'You can't be serious? Who the hell plays poker for *limousines?*' I say in bewilderment, really hoping they're joking.

'Billionaires!' Oliver answers, flipping over a card to reveal the joker. 'You couldn't make it up, could you?'

Feeling rather uncomfortable with the idea of them playing for such ridiculous stakes, I look down at the jumbled cards on the table.

'Here he is now!' Vernon says eagerly, pointing into the distance.

Spinning around, my stomach churns as I spot Stelios and either Ioannis or Georgios walking our way. Waving a set of keys in the air, he grins widely and sprints across the sand.

'There you go, my friend! You win!' Dropping the keys into Marc's hands, Stelios sits down and expertly shuffles the deck of cards. 'Who's in for another game?'

An astounded silence falls across the group as we all stare at the keys.

'Stelios, I can't really accept these.' Marc says, wiggling his fingers so the keys jangle lightly. 'Here, take them back. Put them back in your pocket and we'll have another game...'

'No!' Stelios protests, dealing cards casually. 'I lose, you win! Maybe I win next time. Who knows?'

I peek at Oliver and realise he's watching the scene unfold carefully. His expression gives nothing away as he looks from Stelios to Marc and back again.

'Dude...' Vernon begins, placing a friendly hand on Stelios's back. 'You don't actually have to hand over the keys! It was just banter!'

'Banter?' Stelios repeats, looking up at Ioannis for an explanation and frowning when he translates into Greek.

'No banter! The limousine is yours.' Holding his cards close to his chest, Stelios motions for the others to pick up theirs. 'Any more of this refusal and you will upset me. You will upset me very much. Please, continue.'

Taking the hint that he obviously isn't going to accept his keys back, Marc and Vernon reluctantly pick up their cards. From my place up on the balcony it seemed the guys were having a friendly bonding session, but now I'm in the midst of their game I am seeing it in a whole new light. It feels wrong, it feels false and worst of all, it doesn't feel fun in the slightest.

'Oliver?' Stelios prompts, pushing a set of cards towards him. 'Are you in?'

I hold my breath as Oliver stares at Stelios for a moment too long before nodding.

'I'm in...'

*   *   *

'What's going on up here?' I ask, following the sound of Janie's cackle onto the terrace. 'I could hear you lot down at the beach.'

Discovering Gina, Lianna and Janie drinking from a giant bowl in the centre of the table, I suddenly wish I had stayed with the guys.

'Aris made us some fishbowls!' Lianna manages between slurps, hooting when she makes it to the end of the bowl first.

'Fishbowls?' I repeat, grimacing as memories of teenage trips to Tenerife come flooding back to me. 'Why?'

'It was Gina's idea...' Li explains merrily, diving into a bag of nachos and offering them around the table.

'Ahh...' Not needing any more explanation, I groan as a bartender, who I presume to be Aris, places another enormous bowl on the table.

'I have to say, Janie.' Aris mumbles uncertainly, handing her a selection of foot-long straws. 'This makes a difference to pouring Mr Christopoulos's ouzo of an evening.'

'A good difference?' Janie asks, looking up at Aris and giggling at his appalled expression.

Aris looks over at Gina, who is cheering boisterously and politely excuses himself. Giving him an apologetic smile as he slips back into the building, I resist the urge to run after him. It appears I'm not the only one who doesn't want to be a part of this.

'Alright!' Clapping her hands together, Gina bounces up and down in her seat. 'I'm *definitely* going to win this one!'

'Are you in, Clara?' Lianna asks, twisting a piece of hair around her finger and reaching for a pink straw.

Shaking my head, I turn to leave and stop when Janie tugs on the sleeve of my kaftan.

'Oh, come on!' She says coaxingly, pulling me back towards the table. 'Aris is the best mixologist in Mykonos!'

Glancing at the giant bowl of multi-coloured liquid, I don't have much faith in the lethal concoction tasting anything like the mojito I'm craving right now. The sickening neon potion is making my stomach feel queasy just looking at it. However, knowing they won't give up, I begrudgingly sit down and take a green straw as they whoop happily.

'Three... two... *one!*' Gina yells, causing Li and Janie to start gulping like a pair of hungry fish.

Bracing myself before taking a sip, I immediately recoil and fight the urge to spit into the bowl.

'What the hell is that?' I ask in horror, shuddering at the sour taste.

Not bothering to answer, the three of them race to the bottom until Gina bangs her hand on the table in victory.

'I told you!' She cheers, turning the empty bowl upside down and placing it on her head. 'I've still got it!'

'Is this phase two of the midlife crisis?' I ask jokingly, holding my hand out for a high-five. 'Drinking games?'

Gina's smile freezes at the words *midlife crisis* and I immediately regret bringing it up.

'Midlife crisis?' Taking the bowl off her head, she drops it onto the table with a clatter. 'What midlife crisis? What are you talking about?'

Seemingly losing the ability to speak, I stare at Gina open-mouthed.

'It was a joke!' I reply eventually, hoping she accepts this and moves the conversation along. 'Why so touchy?'

'Because... because I'm hardly *middle-aged*, Clara!' Forcing a strained laugh, Gina dusts an imaginary piece of dust off her shoulder. 'I'm thirty-nine and a whole lot of months. That is *not* middle-aged.'

A little stumped by her overreaction, I look at Lianna for help and frown when she signals that she doesn't want to get involved.

'No, but...'

'But what?' Gina snaps, not missing a beat. 'What are you trying to say? Don't beat around the bush.'

'It's just that you've been letting your hair down an awful lot lately. The drinking on the plane, the old dresses, the tacky tattoos and now *fishbowls?*' Attempting a friendly laugh, I stop when Gina glares back at me. 'Come on! You can see where I'm coming from, right?'

Hearing their tattoos being referred to as *tacky*, Li and Janie join Gina in giving me daggers.

'No.' Gina says seriously. 'I have absolutely no idea what you're talking about.'

Realising the subject of Gina's glaringly obvious midlife crisis is going down like a lead balloon, I try to backtrack. 'I'm kidding! Haven't you known me long enough to know when I'm pulling your leg? Besides, you're way past a midlife crisis. The next thing for you is an *end-of-life* crisis!'

Finally relenting, Gina smiles and nudges my shoulder. 'I should have known you were pulling my leg when you said *tacky tattoo!*'

Breathing a sigh of relief that I seem to have dodged a bullet, I laugh along with the others as they compare their inkings.

'I mean, just look at it!' Gina says, stroking her wrist and beaming brightly. 'It's totally classy, right?'

Crossing my fingers behind my back, I smile back at her and nod in agreement.

'Yes, it is, Gina. Yes, it is...'

Chapter 12

'An actual limo, Marc?' Gina gasps, taking the shiny keys from him and gaping at them in shock. 'You're seriously telling me that you won a *limo?*'

'I know, it's insane, but he just wouldn't take *no* for an answer.' Marc whispers, accepting a canapé from one of the butlers and popping it straight into his mouth. 'The more I tried to give the keys back, the more insulted Stelios became. Like it or not, the limo is now ours.'

I lock eyes with Oliver and hold my glass against my chest. We haven't spoken about the infamous poker game and we don't need to. The way his lip curls up with disdain each and every time the word *limo* is mentioned tells me everything I need to know.

'How the hell are we going to get it home?' Gina's asks, abandoning her drink and jingling the keys in her hand.

'I don't know, but I'll drive it back myself if I have to!' Pushing his glasses up the bridge of his sunburnt nose, Marc laughs and shakes his head. 'We've got a *limo*, Gina!'

The same silly expression that Marc had down on the beach creeps onto Gina's face as she drops the keys into her handbag.

'This is the best holiday *ever!*' Letting out a squeal, Gina stamps her feet excitedly. 'Did you know about this, Clara?'

I nod and step aside as Lianna and Vernon finally join us at the bar. 'I did, but I don't think Lianna does. Why don't you fill her in on the news?'

Picking up my glass, I leave the others to chat and head over to where Aris is expertly pouring drinks by the balcony. My abrupt departure from the group might seem a little rude, but I don't think I can stomach another second of listening to their shrieks of delight. Their acceptance of Stelios's limousine has disappointed me somewhat. I secretly hoped Gina would refuse the outrageous gesture and maintain a little self-respect, but alas, they have done the complete opposite.

'Aris?' I say gently, coming to a stop by the open windows. 'Do you happen to know where Janie is?'

Placing two glasses on the counter, he nods and points down a corridor to our left. 'Janie is preparing herself for dinner in the bedroom.'

Following his gaze, I realise he's pointing to a wing of the villa I am yet to explore. 'And which room would that be, exactly?'

'The sixth door on the left.' Aris replies, stepping out from behind the bar with a silver tray bearing seven flutes of fizz. 'You like me to take you there?'

'I'm sure I'll find it.' I flash him a wink and take another glass from his tray. 'Thank you, Aris.'

'Parakaló...'

Slipping through the many members of staff, who appear to be doing nothing more than straightening already-straight furniture, I slowly walk down the hall and count the doors carefully. The same neutral theme from the guest wing continues throughout the spacious lobby, making the plain walls appear painfully bare. Gentle music from the bar creeps up on me as I study the minimalistic furnishings and nondescript photographs, wondering how a building so prestigious can feel so bleak and vacant.

Pausing to study a painted canvas, I frown at the ivory splashes and try to see something within the random blotches of paint. Just like the rest of the villa, the artwork is empty and insipid, without any depth of character. What you see, is simply what you get. Nothing more and nothing less. There's no hidden meaning, no sense of what inspired the artist, and no secret waiting to be revealed within its beauty. In this place, it seems beauty is most certainly skin-deep.

Walking away from the painting, I stop outside a set of gold doors and knock on the heavy wood. A muffled response comes back at me and I take it as my cue to release the handle.

'Janie?' I whisper, really hoping Stelios isn't going to appear in his birthday suit.

Slowly pushing open the door, I step inside and look around the enormous suite. 'Janie, are you in here?'

Too distracted by the giant regal bed, I almost don't see Janie sitting at a garish metallic dressing table.

'There you are!' I say with a grin, holding out one of the glasses. 'May I come in?'

'It looks like you already are!' Pushing herself up, she accepts the fizz and immediately takes a huge gulp. 'But sure, get in here!'

Smiling back at her, I allow the door to close behind me and marvel at the peculiar interior. Unlike the rest of the building, this grand boudoir has *Janie* written all over it. From the leopard print bedding to the scarlet walls and oversized chandelier. It couldn't reflect more of the Janie we know and love if it tried.

'Wow! It's... *bright* in here.' I muse, choosing my words carefully. 'What a dramatic change from the rest of the place.'

Nodding along, Janie stands back and looks around the bedroom proudly. 'Do you like it?'

'I love it!' I lie, hoping she can't see through my strained smile. 'You've certainly put your own stamp on the place!'

'Believe it or not, this is all Stelios.' She confesses honestly, motioning around the flamboyant room. 'I haven't changed a single thing. Not that I would want to.'

Studying the many portraits of Stelios, I feel my spirits lift as I spot a polaroid of Janie in a heart-shaped frame.

'I knew the sleek and sophisticated look wasn't really Stelios.' I reply, stroking the velvet curtains. 'Why isn't everywhere in this style?'

'Stelios has to keep a level of professionalism at the villa.' Shrugging her shoulders, Janie sits down on the bed. 'He holds the majority of his business negotiations right here in the dining room.'

'So?' I reply, glancing up at the mirrored ceiling and shuddering. 'What does that have to do with anything?'

Pouting her collagen-filled lips, Janie places her glass on the bedside table. 'In this industry, image is everything. Stelios already has a reputation for being a little offbeat. His associates wouldn't be very impressed if they arrived to see personalised thrones and gold statues...'

Following her gaze, I laugh at the sight of two epic thrones with satin cushions.

'I can understand his predicament, but it's a shame Stelios can't be himself in his own home. Being a billionaire should allow you to enjoy such luxury.'

'You'd think...' Janie grumbles.

Taking a seat on the edge of the bed next to her, I hold out my arms to steady myself as the mattress wobbles beneath me.

'It's a water bed.' She explains, rushing to grab my drink before I spill it on the plush carpet. 'Well, I say *water*, but it's actually filled with Champagne.'

'Champagne!' I giggle, kicking off my shoes and shuffling along the mattress. 'Surely even Stelios isn't that ostentatious!'

'I'm being serious!' Janie laughs along with me and throws herself back onto the cushions. 'His doctor insists it's good for his arthritis!'

Not believing that for a second, I bounce up and down and immediately feel seasick. 'Only Stelios Christopoulos could have a Champagne-filled mattress!'

A flicker of annoyance hits Janie's eyes before she replaces it with a smile. 'He can afford to.'

'I know he can *afford* to, but he doesn't *have* to.' Hoping she recognises where I'm coming from, my heart sinks when she stares back at me blankly. 'You do know that Stelios gave Marc a *limo* before, don't you?'

'He did?' Batting her long eyelashes innocently, she frowns and sits up straight. 'Why?'

'Marc won it in a game of poker.' Stopping to assess her reaction, I take a deep breath before continuing. 'Yesterday, he tried to buy The Haven for Li and Vernon and when we first arrived, we were all presented with rubies big enough to be used as doorstops. Don't you think that's a little excessive?'

Nodding slowly, Janie twists a ruby bracelet around her wrist. 'I told Stelios the rubies were a bad idea. He thought they would win everyone over. In fact, he was sure of it.'

'And that they did!' I exclaim, turning around to face her. 'The guys all adore him!'

'They do?' Her face lights up with happiness as she clasps her hands over her heart. 'They really like him?'

'They do, but the thing is, they would love *anyone* who offered to buy them restaurants, showered them with precious gemstones and gave them a limousine in a game of poker.' I say quietly, staring into her eyes.

'What are you saying?' She replies firmly, a tone to her voice that indicates she knows exactly what I am saying.

'The point I am making is that they don't know anything about Stelios. All they know is that he's extraordinarily generous.' Looking down at the ground, I lick my lips before speaking. 'I want them to accept Stelios just as much as you do, but you don't want them to like him purely for his money, do you?'

Janie pauses and strokes the skin surrounding her new tattoo in silence.

'What about Oliver?' She eventually asks, keeping her eyes fixed on the inking.

'What about him?'

'Is there any change in his attitude towards Stelios?' Still not looking me in the eye, Janie swings her legs over the edge of the bed.

'I've tried talking to him, but I won't lie to you, I don't think he's altered his viewpoint at all.' Her pained expression causes my stomach to flip and I decide to hit her with the truth. 'The extravagance isn't helping. I can tell you that much.'

'But, you just told me it's working with the others.' She protests weakly, finally bringing her heavily lined eyes up to meet mine.

'I also told you the reason why...'

The pair of us sit in an awkward stillness, the only sound coming from the ornate grandfather clock.

'Throwing expensive gifts around isn't the right way to make people like you.' I whisper, hearing the music in the bar turn up a notch. 'You don't need me to tell you that...'

'Stelios couldn't spend all of his money if he tried, so he doesn't see it as a big deal.' Janie explains exasperatedly. 'Everyone else loves Stelios for his generosity...'

'Is that why *you* love him?' I ask, cutting her off mid-sentence.

'Yes.' Janie fires back, not hesitating for a millisecond.

Feeling my jaw drop open, I stare at my mother-in-law open-mouthed. We all suspected Janie's draw to Stelios was his bulging bank account, but no one ever expected her to admit it.

'But he's also kind, caring, funny and the most beautiful person I have ever met.' Janie continues, much to my relief. 'Both inside and out.'

Screwing up my nose at that last one, I smile back at my mother-in-law as a sense of pride washes over me. 'You obviously love Stelios and we need to make the others love him too, but not for the numbers in his bank account. They need to fall in love with the man behind the billionaire status. They need to fall in love with Stelios Christopoulos and *not* his mountain of cash.'

Janie nods along and smiles gratefully, visibly blinking back tears.

'But how do we do that?' She asks, clearing her throat and shaking off the unusual emotion she's displaying. 'You're only here for three more days.'

'It's not going to be easy.' Considering her question, I tap my fingers on the duvet and look around the bedroom for ideas. 'Oliver's going to take the most work, because to him, Stelios has a hell of a lot more to prove. You're his mother, he just wants the best for you. Even though he doesn't always show it, he does.'

'What if he doesn't change his mind? What if he *never* approves of Stelios?' She asks, her eyes glassing over once more. 'Just yesterday, you said it would be a piece of cake. Now you don't sound so sure.'

Looking out of the window at the black ocean, I feel doubt hit my stomach. 'We can't physically force Oliver to accept Stelios. We just have to let him come to the realisation himself... with a little *encouragement* along the way.'

'Encouragement.' Janie says slowly, like this is the answer she has been searching for all along. 'Yeah. Maybe you're right. Perhaps Oliver just needs a little nudge in the right direction to see Stelios for who he truly is.'

'Exactly!' Suddenly feeling rather optimistic, I clink my glass against hers and take a deep gulp. 'Just think, if Stelios is as marvellous a person as it seems, how could he possibly not?'

Chapter 13

Catching Janie's eye across the colossal dining table, I offer her a discreet wink and rest my head on Oliver's shoulder. The laughter of my best friends surrounds me as I rub my stomach, making me feel more relaxed than I have all holiday. For the past couple of hours, we have consumed more calories than I knew was humanly possible, guzzled a ludicrous amount of alcohol and chatted to our heart's content. Even Oliver managed to raise a smile as we shared stories and tales of days gone by.

Looking up at him as he relaxes in his seat, I feel more confident than ever that I'll be able to get him cheering for *Team Stelios*. After all, apart from being a little ostentatious and sometimes a tad irritating with his flashy ways, Stelios hasn't done a single thing to deserve Oliver's loathing of him. Yes, his incessant need to show his wealth might be misconstrued as showy, but the guy *is* a billionaire. He was hardly going to live in a two-up two-down and drive a battered old Mondeo, was he?

With the Ice Party taking place on Friday, I have just two free days left to change Oliver's opinion on his mother's choice of partner. Hopefully, my earlier conversation with Janie will have put a stop to Stelios's outlandish displays of prosperity and will give Oliver a chance to see beyond the pantomime. Glimpsing at Stelios as he leads the conversation from the head of the table, I notice how his eyes sparkle with sheer joy when he realises Janie is looking on lovingly as he speaks.

How can Oliver not see what an amazing influence Stelios has been on his mother? Every sharp edge that once defined the boisterous Janie has been softened, revealing a woman who I am proud to barely recognise. After a tempestuous dating history and a somewhat turbulent few years since her divorce from Oliver's father, it seems Janie has finally found her feet... and a good man to keep her on them.

'I think I'm going to call it a night.' Mark announces, yawning into his sleeve. 'I'm absolutely exhausted.'

'Don't be such a party pooper!' Ruffling his hair, Gina reaches for the wine bottle and frowns when she discovers it's empty. 'The night's still young!'

Marc groans and takes off his glasses to rub his tired eyes, signalling he's going to hit the hay regardless.

Realising I could use this time to my advantage, I discreetly nudge Janie to get her attention.

'Let's stay up a while and chat. We never just chat anymore.' I say cheerily, giving Janie a knowing look. 'Stelios, why don't you tell us a little about yourself? Who is Stelios Christopoulos?'

'Are you kidding me?' Gina groans, before Stelios can answer. 'We've been chatting for the last three hours! Let's go dancing!'

Not wanting to lose the chance to delve further into Stelios's life and reveal a side to him Oliver might warm to, I shake my head in response.

'What do you say, Stelios?' She persists, dancing around in her seat. 'You can tell a lot about a man by the way he moves on the dance floor!'

Clearly not wanting to disappoint Gina, Stelios laughs nervously and glances at Janie for help.

'You can tell even more about a man by asking him about his life.' Janie says with a smile, picking up on my lead.

'Come on, Stelios, tell us about yourself.' I say happily, quickly jumping on the subject before Gina can talk Calix into driving her to a nightclub.

'What do you want to know?' Smiling merrily, Stelios sits up straight and looks around the table. 'Ask me anything! Anything at all. Nothing is off-limits for my family!'

Hoping this is the moment that we will get to see the real Stelios, I subtly give Janie the thumbs-up sign as Stelios braces himself for the first question.

'How much money do you have in your pocket right now?' Vernon asks, to Lianna's horror.

'*Vernon!* Don't be so rude!' She hisses. 'I'm so sorry, Stelios. Don't answer that.'

Not flinching, Stelios reaches into his pocket and drops a wad of notes onto the table. Slowly removing the ruby-encrusted clip, he flicks through the cash at ease.

'Two thousand euro. I no carry much cash. All cards.' Placing the money back into his pocket casually, he awaits the next question.

'How much is Ianthe worth?' Marc whispers, his cheeks flushing when Gina glares at him.

Letting out a groan, I hold my head in my hands. When Stelios said nothing was off-limits, I don't think he was including the figures on his bank statements. Why do they think it's acceptable to pry into Stelios's financial affairs just because he has tons of cash?

'Where did you grow up, Stelios?' I ask, ensuring my voice is louder than everyone else's.

Seemingly relieved to be getting away from the subject of money, Stelios smiles thankfully.

'I grew up right here. Mykonos is my hometown.' Taking Janie's hand, he holds it over his heart. 'Mykonos is where my heart is.'

'So, are your parents here in Mykonos?' I continue, attempting to keep the conversation on track.

'My mother, yes.' Stelios says fondly, clutching his medallion. 'My father, he... he passed on.'

'I'm very sorry to hear that.' Lianna replies tactfully. 'Are you close with your mother?'

'Very!' Janie answers on his behalf. 'Just like me and Oliver! Isn't that right, son?'

Oliver manages a tiny nod in response and smiles, but I notice him tense in his seat.

'I am glad you mention my mother.' Stelios says, breaking into a huge grin once more. 'My mother is joining us for brunch tomorrow.'

'She is?' I reply, intrigued to meet the woman who created the man with a love for leopard print and red velvet. 'That's so lovely! I can't wait to meet her.'

'And she cannot wait to meet all of you!' Clapping his hands together, Stelios sighs theatrically and pulls Janie towards him. 'My mother is very much looking forward to meeting you. You're all my family now. Tomorrow we unite as one big family.'

I smile back at him and steal a glimpse at the others. Surprisingly, they don't look half as alarmed as I would expect them to. It appears the *my family* referrals are starting to lose effect.

'Thank you all for your company this evening.' Pushing out his chair, Stelios bows his head and holds out his hand for Janie's. 'Tomorrow, the Christopoulos family and the Jones family unite as one. Until then, I bid you goodnight!'

With a final wave, Stelios and Janie sashay through the foyer, leaving the rest of us staring at where they once sat. Waiting for them to disappear out of sight, I open my mouth to suggest we all retire too, but Gina beats me to it.

'Who the hell are the Jones family?' She asks, swirling the remnants of her wine around her glass.

'That's Janie's maiden name.' I explain, keeping my voice down in case they return.

'And who are her family?' Gina persists.

'Us, apparently.' Vernon laughs and turns to look at the calm ocean outside. 'Not that I'm complaining. If Stelios wants me to be a Jones, I'll be a Jones!'

'I second that!' Marc hoots, draining his glass and standing to his feet. 'I'll be Fred freaking Flintstone, if he wants me to be!'

A laugh titters around the room as the rest of them nod in agreement.

'Anyway, Fred Flintstone, it's been a lovely evening, but it's way past my bedtime.' Lianna mumbles, pushing out her chair. 'I'm going to bed.'

Swiftly finishing her drink, Lianna showers us all with kisses before heading in the direction of the guest wing with Vernon in tow.

'So, Oliver, what's it going to take to get you to crack a smile?' Marc teases, taking a crumpled napkin from the table and folding it neatly. 'A helicopter? Your name carved in gold? The entire freaking island?'

'There isn't enough money in all of Greece to win me over.' Shaking his head, Oliver laughs lightly. 'Pigs will fly before I give her my blessing to be with Stelios.'

Silently groaning, I try to hide my disappointment. At this rate, Oliver is never going to accept Stelios. Encouragement or no encouragement.

'That's a bit harsh.' Marc replies, giving Oliver a friendly nudge. 'He's a good guy. Trust me, I have a good gut instinct about these things.'

'Would you want him to be with *your* mom?' Oliver snaps. 'You show me a man who would be happy to see his mom with Stelios Christopoulos and I'll show you a liar.'

Marc taps his foot as he thinks, until Oliver nods and finishes his drink.

'Exactly. On that note, I'm going to bed.' Kissing my cheek, Oliver waves to the others. 'Goodnight, guys.'

'Goodnight!' Marc and Gina shout after him.

Watching him leave, I tip back my head and whimper. Winning over Oliver is going to be a lot harder than I anticipated. With just three days to go, the chances of this ending with happily ever after are getting lower by the second.

'So, it's just us three left standing!' Gina chirps, drumming her hands on the table. 'Who's up for dancing?'

Marc and I share a look and I shake my head.

'We're meeting Stelios's mother tomorrow. I don't think it's a good idea to paint the town red tonight.' Discreetly moving Vernon's glass of wine away from her, I stifle a yawn. 'Save your dancing for the Ice Party.'

'Seriously?' Gina's face falls with disappointment and she stamps her feet like a petulant child. 'This is supposed to be a holiday!'

'It *is* a holiday!' Marc chuckles, wrapping his arms around her. 'But you've already done enough *holidaying* for all of us!'

Rolling her eyes, Gina wiggles out of Marc's grip and grabs her drink. 'I didn't realise I was married to a pensioner.'

'I think you'll find you're older than me!' He retorts, laughing as she stumbles towards the guest wing with the wine glass still in her hand. 'Goodnight, honey!'

Grumbling under her breath in response, Gina flips Marc the bird and makes her way to her bedroom.

'And then there were two!' Marc says, walking around the immense dining room and admiring the artwork I snubbed earlier.

'I hate to disappoint you, but I think they'll be just one very shortly!' I confess, yawning into my cloth napkin. 'I can barely keep my eyes open.'

'You're all gone!' Aris exclaims, stepping into the room with a tray of wine glasses. 'Why?'

'Everyone's gone to bed.' I explain, making a sleep sign with my hands. 'They're all sleeping.'

'Ah! I see...' Looking down at the glasses in disappointment, Aris frowns and shrugs his shoulders. 'No problem. I take these back.'

Turning around, Aris takes a few steps towards the bar area before stopping and looking over his shoulder. 'Unless, you want one last drink?'

I look up at Marc and smile when I see he is already reaching out his hand.

'Thanks, Aris. I suppose one more can't hurt.' Accepting a glass, I thank Aris once more and follow Marc out onto the terrace.

'Famous last words...' Marc chuckles, wandering around the huge infinity pool.

'Should I go and get Gina?' Enjoying the sound of crickets chirping all around us, I dip a toe into the cold water. 'She will be livid if she finds out we have been drinking without her!'

'Leave her to sleep. She could do with an early night.' He replies, turning a chair to face the moon and sitting down. 'I don't know what's got into her on this trip. She's been acting like the crazy Gina she was when we first met. Must be the ouzo...'

Spotting this as my chance to broach the subject of Gina's midlife crisis, I take a big swig from my glass before sitting down next to him.

'She's certainly letting her hair down, isn't she?' I say casually, watching the moonlight glimmer on the surface of the ocean. 'If I didn't know any better, I would say she's on the verge of a midlife crisis...'

Looking at me over the rim of his glass, Marc promptly erupts into hysterics. 'Don't be ridiculous!'

'I'm being serious! You should be worried about what's coming next.' I reply sternly, trying to keep a straight face. 'You won't be laughing when she gets a tongue piercing, or worse!'

'She's not having a midlife crisis, Andrews!' Marc scoffs running his fingers through his hair.

Not being convinced, I raise my eyebrows tellingly and shrug. 'I wouldn't be so sure. If I were you, I would keep an eye on her.'

'Listen, you don't need to worry about that.' Dismissing my concerns with a flick of his hand, Marc scratches his stubble. 'What you *do* need to worry about, is Oliver.'

My ears prick up at the mention of Oliver and I put down my glass. 'What about Oliver?'

'Janie has struck gold here with Stelios. Literally, gold.' Marc's eyes glisten at the word *gold*, giving me a clue as to the direction in which this conversation is going. 'Don't let Oliver ruin it by driving a wedge between them. His hostility towards Stelios is impossible to ignore and if we can feel it, Stelios will, too.'

'I know!' I cry, glad to have someone to talk to about this. 'I completely understand Oliver's reservations...'

'I bloody don't!' Marc interrupts, laughing sarcastically. 'Just think about it. Stelios doesn't have any children. If he goes on to marry Janie and I'm pretty confident he will, this whole thing will be Oliver's one day.'

Looking deep into Marc's eyes as he speaks, I feel my stomach churn.

'It will be *both* of yours.' He whispers, looking around the sprawling terrace. 'Do you realise what an opportunity this is? You've won the lottery!'

'But... but that's not the point, is it?' Hoping Aris can't overhear our conversation, I shuffle closer to Marc. 'It doesn't matter whether Stelios is rich or poor, the money doesn't come into it. Oliver has his reservations based on Stelios's turbulent past relationships and his reputation for being an unscrupulous businessman. It's not like Oliver is judging him without reason. Yes, Stelios has been nothing but lovely to us, but I can appreciate why

Oliver is having a hard time leaving the past in the past.'

Shaking his head, Marc drapes his arm around the back of his seat. 'This isn't a standard case of boy doesn't like mummy's new boyfriend though, is it? He has to look at the bigger picture here. This is a once in a lifetime opportunity for all of us.'

'For all of us?' I repeat apprehensively, staring into the bottom of my glass.

'Yes, all of us! Clara, we've been given rubies and limousines. I've played golf with some of the most powerful men in the business. Li and Vernon nearly had a damn restaurant bought for them.' Reaching into his pocket, Marc places the sparkling ruby on the table between us. 'What does it matter if Stelios has a sleazy past? Surely his extreme generosity buys him a little leeway on all that stuff?'

Picking up the ruby, I turn it over in my hands and study my reflection in the polished stone.

'You do think Stelios is good for Janie though, don't you, Marc?' I ask, bringing my eyes up to meet his. 'If we would have arrived to a shack and a few mattresses on the floor, you would still be telling me this?'

Marc gives me a look that answers my question perfectly and I hang my head. The idea of him liking Stelios purely for his money fills me with sadness. While Janie is desperate to get everyone's approval of her relationship, the guys have been lapping up Stelios's attempts at getting them on his side without a second thought to his intentions. It would appear that once the cash comes out to play, Stelios could reveal himself as a serial killer and they still wouldn't care.

'But what if he isn't right for Janie?' I whisper, keeping one eye on Aris as he clears away the empty glasses in the dining room. 'What if Oliver is right and Stelios *is* bad news? What if Janie is risking her relationship with Oliver for a man who simply views her as a bit of fun? What if...'

'What if *nothing*.' Marc says with a laugh. 'We could all say *what if* with our relationships. We could all say *what if* one hundred times a day, but we don't. We simply trust our gut and go with it.'

Not knowing quite what I want to say, I turn to look at the water and take a deep breath.

'Just think, Stelios could get bored of Janie at any moment. He might roll out of bed tomorrow and decide he's had enough of her and move on to the next thing that catches his eye. Just as easily as Janie could get bored of him.' Marc persists, tugging on my arm to get my attention. 'There's no guarantee with any relationship, so don't try and pick it apart to find one. Just enjoy this while it lasts. Live for today and forget about what, why and how. None of that matters.'

Marc's words whirl around my mind and a whole new wave of doubt hits me. I'm sure he's trying to reassure me, but all he is doing is making me feel worse.

'What if this is all just a game to Stelios?' I think aloud, an awful sensation hitting my stomach.

'Exactly! That's what I've been trying to tell you.' Picking up the ruby from the centre of the table, Marc tosses it into the air and catches it effortlessly. 'There's every chance Stelios and Janie are the real deal, but this might just as easily be a flash in the pan romance.'

Knowing from my secret chats with Janie she is most certainly *not* viewing this relationship as temporary in any way, shape or form, I bite my lip nervously. Janie is laying her cards on the table, she has her skin in the game, but all that could mean nothing if Stelios is playing a different game entirely.

'No offence, Andrews, but Stelios Christopoulos could have his pick of all the women in Greece. He has absolutely nothing to gain by choosing Janie. Don't be too upset if this doesn't work out as you hope.' Marc says seriously, keeping his gaze fixed on mine. 'Which brings me back to my initial point. Don't think too hard about the dynamics of this relationship. *Just enjoy it while it lasts.*'

Nodding in response, I clutch my glass to my chest and stare at the deserted beach below.

I've been so consumed with not allowing Oliver to ruin this for Janie that I haven't taken a moment to think about the possibility of this not being the happy ending she's hoping for. I want to believe the only thing standing in her way is Oliver's refusal to see her as her own woman, a woman who makes her own decisions, but what if Janie's happily ever after is purely one-sided? When we first arrived here in Mykonos, I was confident this relationship was as permanent as the ouzo in Stelios's cabinet, but now I am not so sure.

'Sometimes, you have to see the good and ignore the bad.' He continues calmly, motioning around the balcony once more. 'Selective blindness isn't always a bad thing.'

Trying to decipher his riddle, I manage a tiny smile as he ruffles my hair before pushing out his chair and heading back inside.

'Goodnight, Andrews.' He shouts over his shoulder, the sound of his footsteps fading into the distance.

'Marc?' I yell after him, wandering over to the open door.

Stopping in his tracks, Marc turns around and smiles. 'Yes?'

Hesitating for a moment, I open my mouth to say something, but decide against it at the last second.

'Nothing. Goodnight...'

Chapter 14

Studying the heap of discarded clothing on the bed, I rifle through my collection of dresses in search of the perfect outfit. The once immaculate suite is now littered with shoes, handbags and various clothes that have either been deemed inappropriate, unsuitable or more simply put – just not good enough.

Tapping my foot impatiently, I kick a pile of shorts in frustration and throw open the wardrobe. Stelios's mother shall be here at any moment for brunch down on the beach, yet apart from a black thong and a slick of red lipstick, I am completely naked. Pretty confident she isn't going to want to see me in all my glory, I pluck a blush-coloured sundress from the rack and slip it over my head.

After my late-night conversation with Marc yesterday, I didn't sleep a wink. For hours on end I tossed and turned as I listened to the sound of the waves crashing against the beach outside the window. No matter how hard I tried to shake them off, Marc's words rang in my ears all night long.

Sometimes, you have to see the good and ignore the bad.

They say ignorance is bliss, but where do you draw the line? Just how much should we choose to ignore? Where does ignorance stop and acceptance of what is wrong begin? The politics of relationships have always been somewhat of a mystery to me, but when they involve two people as eccentric as Janie and Stelios, they become even more complicated.

Grabbing a floppy hat from my suitcase, I brush my hair out of my face and reach for my sandals. The rest of the gang have been waiting on the beach for the past thirty minutes and if I waste a moment longer thinking about Marc's words of warning, I will undoubtedly be rebuked when I eventually make an appearance. Refusing to look in the mirror in case I deem this outfit for the scrapheap too, I slip on my sunglasses and make my way down to the beach.

Despite the size of Stelios's palatial mansion, I am finding my way around the place incredibly well and as a result, I make it to the others in five minutes flat.

'Wow! This looks amazing!' I gush, taking a seat at a beautifully dressed table and admiring the display.

The long table is covered with a delicate white cloth, which is gently billowing in the sea breeze. Numerous pearlescent vases display beautiful bouquets of flowers, making the whole scene appear more fitting for an elaborate wedding than a simple morning brunch. Hoping this exorbitant display is a sign of how much Stelios wants this meeting to be a success, I smile at Janie and take a picture of the stunning presentation on my phone.

'You look nice.' Oliver whispers, reaching for my hand across the table and wrapping his fingers around mine. 'You were worth the wait.'

Beaming back at him, I notice his smile reach his eyes for the first time on this holiday. His dark curls are effortlessly brushed back as he rhythmically rubs his thumb over my index finger. As I lose myself in his eyes, my conversation with Marc comes flooding back to me once more and I steal a glimpse at Janie's unconventional choice of partner.

Stelios is practically glowing and so is Janie. To any passer-by, they look the perfect image of togetherness, but what if Stelios's grand gestures are nothing out of the ordinary? What if this is simply how Stelios treats every notch on his bedpost? What if Janie is preparing to commit her life to someone who is simply having some fun before moving onto the next? Half of me thinks it's incredibly far-fetched to believe Stelios would go to such lengths for someone he didn't have genuine feelings for, but when money is of no value to a person, how can you know if what they're offering is real?

I don't want to believe Marc is right. I, more than anyone, want this to be Janie's fairy tale ending and until my chat with Marc last night, I genuinely did believe it was. In spite of Marc's thoughts on their relationship, there's a lot of evidence to suggest the contrary. After all, they've been together for almost a year now. If this was nothing more than a meaningless tryst to Stelios, surely the novelty would have worn off by now. Wouldn't it?

Not knowing what to think anymore, I try to push it to the back of my mind and turn my focus to Lianna.

'What have I missed?' I ask, admiring her polka dot skirt and crop top combination.

'Not much.' Turning her back to the wind, Li takes a rose from one of the vases and holds it to her nose. 'We took some photographs, Gina and I went for a stroll along the shore... oh, and Stelios bought everyone speedboats.'

'You mean, he's taking everyone speedboating?' I reply, fidgeting with my watch.

'Nope.' Reaching for the breadbasket, Li pops a seeded baguette onto her plate. 'He's bought us all actual speedboats. Don't worry, you have one, too.'

She points to a row of twinkling speedboats and I'm hit with a sense of immense frustration. Clearly my conversation with Janie regarding Stelios flashing the cash fell on deaf ears.

Before I can tell her I don't want a bloody speedboat, I'm interrupted by a loud cheering from further along the shore. Looking past Lianna, I spot a tiny old lady, wearing far too many layers for the warm weather, waving her arms around in the air.

'*Ma!*' Stelios cries suddenly, diving out of his seat and racing across the hot sand.

Flanked by two enormous minders, Konstantina Christopoulos appears the height of a small child as she feebly holds onto Stelios's arm and makes a beeline for Janie. Watching the two of them trudge along the shore, I remark at how much they look alike. If you ignore the huge pearls, floral headscarf and pink lipstick, Konstantina is Stelios's doppelganger.

'My Janie!' Konstantina croons, wrapping her incredibly brown arms around Janie's neck. 'My beautiful Janie!'

Suddenly aware of where Stelios gets his extreme friendliness from, I rest my elbows on the table and watch as Konstantina cups her wrinkly hands around Janie's face. Her eyes light up as she kisses both of Janie's cheeks twice over, before pulling her in for yet another hug.

'They certainly seem close!' Li whispers, standing up as Janie leads Konstantina our way. 'If I didn't know any better, I would believe she was Janie's mother, not Stelios's.'

Nodding in agreement, I smooth down my hair and position myself next to Lianna.

'Konni, this is my son, Oliver.' Janie says proudly, coming to a stop next to Oliver's seat and gently pushing Konstantina forward.

'*Oliver!*' Konstantina repeats, flashing him a toothless grin.

'It's a pleasure to meet you, Konstantina.' Standing up to greet her, Oliver appears startled when she yanks him towards her and attacks his cheeks with pink kisses.

'Konni. No Konstantina.' She protests, straightening Oliver's collar before turning back to Janie. 'He big boy. Big and strong. No like mine.'

Oliver blushes and I let out a giggle as Stelios mutters something in Greek at his mother. I don't know what's more hilarious. Oliver being referred to as a big strong boy or Konni pointing out that Stelios is little more than four feet high.

'He look like you.' Konni chuckles, tapping Oliver's stomach and adjusting her headscarf. 'Panemorfi!'

'That's my boy!' Janie says happily, giving Oliver's arm a squeeze as Konni treats the others to sloppy kisses of their own.

Finally dragging herself away from admiring Lianna's hair, Konni turns her attention to me.

'And you! You must be Clara.' Konni says softly, holding out her arms. 'My Janie, she tell me so much about you!'

Giving Janie a sideways glance, I offer Konni my cheek as she studies my face closely. 'You have good heart, Clara. Very good heart.'

'Oh!' I reply, a little taken aback. 'Thank you.'

As Konni is led to her seat by Stelios, I take the opportunity to give her a quick once-over. With Stelios being at least seventy years old, it makes sense to assume that Konni would be around ninety, but even though it isn't possible, she could be double that. Her olive skin is wrinkled beyond recognition and the three teeth she has left are holding on by a thread. Strangely, her brown eyes sparkle like those of a teenager, giving her the mischievous look that is usually reserved for sassy adolescents.

'Very nice to see your people, my Janie.' Looking up at Janie lovingly, Konni reaches for her hand. 'Your people are my people.'

'*Our* people.' Janie corrects.

'Yes, *our* people!' Cheering loudly, Konni adjusts her headscarf and smiles at the rest of us. 'You all our people.'

Smiling as I retreat to my seat, I watch Janie ensure Konni is comfortable before sitting down herself. Placing a napkin over Konni's lap, Janie kisses her cheek as Stelios instructs his waiters to start service.

Waiting until the drinks have been poured and our plates have been dressed with an array of croissants, exotic fruits and pastries, I take a gulp of water and turn to Konni.

'It's so nice that you and Janie have built up such a strong bond.' I say with a smile, jabbing a strawberry with my fork. 'It's really endearing.'

'What she say?' Konni mumbles to Stelios, holding a hand to her ear as Stelios promptly translates. 'Oh, yes! My Janie is the daughter I never had.'

'That's so lovely!' I reply, completely bowled over by Konni's great love for Janie.

The rest of the group, minus Oliver, murmur in agreement as Janie beams brightly from her place next to Stelios.

'So, I'm guessing Janie and Stelios get your blessing, Konni?' Gina asks, tearing apart a croissant and winking at Janie across the table.

'Many girlfriends, my Stelios had. Many, many, many...' Konni says seriously, banging her fist on the table as she speaks. 'No one compares to my Janie. My Janie is the best!'

'The very best!' Stelios adds, wrapping his arms around both of them. 'I have the best girls in all of Greece.'

'Awwh!' Lianna gushes, popping a grape into her mouth. 'I'm so very happy for you both. We all are. Right, guys?'

As Lianna and Gina fire a dozen questions at Konni about her feelings towards Janie, I can't shake Konni's words from my mind.

Many, many, many girlfriends.

Apart from a brief romance with a near-teenager in Florida and numerous one-night stands, this is Janie's first relationship since her divorce from Randy. I really hope Stelios is in this for the long run, as you only need to look at Janie to see she's put everything she has and more into this relationship. Peeking at Oliver out of the corner of my eye, I just know he's thinking it, too.

'So, Stelios has had a lot of women?' Oliver asks boldly, causing me to almost choke on my melon balls.

'Too many!' Konni replies with a laugh, not flinching in the slightest. 'I lose count after one hundred.'

Lianna gives me a subtle nudge and I look over at Stelios, who simply shrugs and reaches for his water.

'What can I say? Women love me!' He jokes teasingly, causing Vernon and Marc to erupt into hysterics.

'He's a man for the ladies, that's for sure!' Vernon chuckles, tapping his glass against Stelios's. 'You've still got it, dude!'

'He certainly has!' Janie purrs. 'I'm a very lucky lady.'

'And *I* am a very lucky man.' Taking Janie's hand in his, Stelios stares into her eyes intently and slowly reaches into his pocket.

The table falls into a stunned silence as he fumbles around inside his jacket, before pulling out a napkin and dabbing his brow. Breathing a sigh of relief that there isn't a diamond ring in there, I attack my food with my fork.

'I thought I was onto a winner there.' Gina whispers, causing Oliver to glare back at her. 'But there's still time yet...'

Shoving a piece of croissant into Oliver's mouth before he can respond, I make a stab at changing the subject.

'Have you ever been to England, Konni?' I ask, pleased to see she seems oblivious to Oliver's bad attitude.

'Yes.' Smiling sweetly, Konni places down her cutlery and rests her hands on the table. 'My Stavros, he is in England.'

'Is Stavros your boyfriend?' Vernon jokes, already knowing Stavros is her other son.

'No!' Laughing rowdily, Konni shakes her head and bats Vernon's arm. 'My boyfriend is *Andreas*.'

We all join in with her laughter and return to our brunch, impressed at Konni's ability to crack a joke.

'Andreas is my mother's third boyfriend.' Stelios explains blankly, holding up three fingers. 'She has many boyfriends, but Andreas is my personal favourite. He's a good boy. Very good.'

Now, I am not ageist, but the idea of toothless, ninety-year-old Konni Christopoulos having three boyfriends is a little hard to believe.

'My mother has, how you say, polyamorous relationships.' Stelios continues, without a hint of a blush. 'Three boyfriends, all very happy.'

Pausing with my fork to my mouth, I look over at Janie for confirmation and raise my eyebrows when she nods to confirm what Stelios is saying is true. Wow. Knock me down with a feather. I'm beginning to discover Konni and Janie might have more in common than I first thought, a *lot* more. Maybe Konni's approval of Janie isn't so hard to believe after all.

'What about you, Stelios?' Oliver asks, staring at him intensely. 'Do *you* have *polyamorous* relations?'

'Before, yes.' Stelios says truthfully, wrapping an arm around Janie's waist. 'But now, no. My Janie is the only woman for me.'

'What makes Janie so special?' Moving her seat closer to Marc, Gina smiles at Stelios. 'Why give up a bachelor's life for our Janie?'

Seemingly lost for words, Stelios plants a kiss on Janie's cheek and sighs melodramatically. 'There are simply no words to describe why my Janie means so much. The dictionary just is not big enough...'

As Stelios continues to rave about Janie, I excuse myself to go to the bathroom. Dropping my napkin next to my plate, I ignore the scowl from Oliver for abandoning him and head for the stone staircase. The strong sun burns down onto my neck as I hitch up my dress and make the short trip back to the villa.

Removing my sunglasses, I smile as I find Calix reading a newspaper on the terrace.

'Hi, Calix!'

'My apologies!' He stammers, hastily jumping to his feet and abandoning his newspaper. 'I was taking a break. What can I do for you?'

'Please don't get up on my account. I'm just nipping to the bathroom.' Signalling for him to sit back down, I continue on my way before stopping when a thought suddenly hits me.

'Calix?' I say quietly, pausing in the doorway. 'Do you have a moment?'

'Of course.' Placing his newspaper on the floor, Calix nods and taps the bench next to him.

I crack my knuckles nervously and gingerly take a seat. 'I want to ask you about Stelios.'

Calix breaks into a huge grin at the mention of Stelios's name and he nods animatedly. 'Ask away. I have worked for Mr Christopoulos for many years now. I know everything there is to know about Stelios.'

Although this is exactly what I wanted him to say, my stomach churns with dread at the prospect of discovering something I don't want to hear.

'What is Stelios like?' I ask, looking around the terrace to ensure we are completely alone. 'I know the man he portrays himself to be, but who is Stelios really? There isn't a single trace of his personality or an insight into his life in this entire place. Apart from his personal bedroom, it's like he doesn't even live here. This villa could be a showroom.'

Slowly nodding, Calix shrugs his shoulders and exhales slowly. 'Stelios is very... *private* person. He keeps cards close to his chest.'

'Private?' I repeat, not willing to accept that many people would use the word *private* to describe Stelios. 'He doesn't seem very private.'

'Oh, he is.' Calix says assuredly. 'Mr Christopoulos never lets you know what is going on up here.' Tapping his forehead, Calix gives me a knowing wink and folds his arms. 'Stelios is expert poker player. Everything is a game to him and he must win. Stelios, he never lose. Not once.'

Allowing his words to sink in, I tap my fingers on the bench thoughtfully.

'Is he a nice man to work for?' I ask. 'Does he treat you well?'

'Mr Christopoulos treats me very well.' Calix says confidently, his face suddenly serious. 'I have no bad words for Stelios.'

Still not satisfied that Stelios's intentions are good, I try to steer the chat down another avenue. 'Has Stelios has many girlfriends?'

'Oh, Stelios has had many, many girlfriends.' Calix giggles and leans back onto the cushions. '*So* many!'

'He has?' I reply, my mind drifting back to when Konni said the same thing down on the beach.

'Very many!' Laughing as he speaks, Calix loosens his collar. 'Stelios is always with girlfriend. One to the next to the next...'

'Wow!' I whisper, trying not to show how much this piece of information bothers me. 'Does Stelios treat Janie any differently to these other girlfriends? He certainly seems to be taken with her.'

'Taken?' Calix repeats, frowning in confusion.

'With all the gifts and introducing her to his mother.' I explain. 'He seems very keen on her.'

'Oh, I understand now.' Rubbing his hands together, Calix shakes his head. 'Stelios is very wealthy man. Stelios spends a lot of money on *all* women. He has so much and it makes him happy to buy things for other people. So, why not?'

'Why not...' I repeat, walking over to the balustrade and watching the others eat their brunch on the beach down below.

Their laughter drifts along the sand, making the whole scene appear the epitome of family togetherness. It's like an idyllic postcard of the perfect holiday. Glasses are clinking together merrily, happy chatter fills the air and smiles are fixed on all but one face as waiters attend to their every need. But something feels off, wrong, somehow, and yet I can't quite pinpoint what exactly it is.

'Has Stelios introduced any other women to his mother?' I ask, watching Janie hug Konni closely.

Joining me by the railing, Calix fixes his gaze on the beach.

'All of them.' He says quietly, not taking his eyes off Stelios. 'Stelios falls in love very quickly and back out of love just as fast. These women, they come and go like the wind. *He loves me, love me not.* Same story every time.'

Obviously recognising the look of alarm on my face, Calix rests a reassuring hand on my arm.

'But please, be certain Mr Christopoulos cares for Janie very much. I can promise you that.' Keeping a serious expression on his face, Calix smiles thinly and places his hands in a prayer pose. 'This time, I hope and pray he has found the right woman...'

*   *   *

Letting the ocean wash over my toes, I watch my pink toenails sparkle beneath the clear water and try to commit the moment to memory. In just forty-eight hours, our Mykonos adventure shall be over and we will be back on home soil. The sand will be shaken from our flip-flops and our suitcases will be locked away until the next voyage. Not wanting to give up on my vacation just yet, I roll onto my stomach as the heat from the sun wraps around my body, reminding me there's still time left to enjoy Greece and all that it has to offer.

Reaching for my cocktail, I look around the beach and smile at the many sun-seeking holidaymakers, each one sprawled out on the powder-soft sand. They look like prawns on a barbecue, just waiting to be drenched in oil and cooked to a golden perfection.

A sudden wave crashes over my legs, soaking me with salty water as I throw myself back on the sand. Courtesy of Stelios, the guys have been whisked away by Calix to watch football at a bar further along the shore. I fully expected Oliver to decline, but to my surprise, he instantly accepted and off in the limo they went. Ever since, Gina, Lianna and I have been toasting ourselves on the beach.

With the guys happily watching their beloved football and Janie enjoying a glass of ouzo at the villa with Konni, it seemed the perfect opportunity to sit back, relax and enjoy the island.

'Do you want to go for a walk?' Lianna asks, rubbing her annoyingly flat stomach and yawning. 'I'm going to fall asleep again if I stay here any longer.'

'Go on then.' Pushing myself up, I grab my kaftan from the lounger behind me and slip it over my wet swimming costume.

'I'm coming, too.' Gina adds, abandoning her beach towel. 'Where are we going?'

Glancing at Lianna for an answer, I follow her as she walks towards the water.

'I don't know.' She mumbles, twisting her hair into a messy bun on the top of her head. 'Left or right?'

Resting my hands on my hips, I take a step back as a family pad across the sand in front of me. To the left, the beach stretches out around a cobbled bay, before trickling off into the water. To the right, a pebbled path leads the way to a bunch of iconic white buildings and traditional cafes.

'Right?' I suggest, pointing at the pretty structures.

Not bothering to respond, Gina and Lianna automatically set off walking in the direction I am indicating.

As we make our way along the shore, we fall into a comfortable quietness and soak up the atmosphere. The breeze that has provided a lovely cooling sensation all afternoon has subsided and all that's left is a warm haze of sunshine. Slipping down the straps on my kaftan, I pause to dip my toes in the ocean. A tiny fish races past my foot, enticing me into the water with a splash of silver as it disappears into the depths of the ocean. Resisting the urge to dive straight in, I force myself to carry on walking and quickly catch up with the others.

'Can you believe this is Janie's life?' Lianna muses, bending down and drawing a line in the sand with her finger. 'After Texas, Florida and London, who would have thought she would find herself here? She certainly landed on her feet, that's for sure.'

My stomach flips as I recall my chat with Calix earlier. Janie has uprooted her entire life. She has moved away from her friends and her family to be with a man her son detests. What if it is all for nothing? Usually, I feel like I am a great judge of character, but what if I am wrong? What if Oliver is right? What if *Calix* is wrong and Stelios is going to move on to someone else very shortly?

Thinking back to my talk with Marc only adds to my concern. Marc was adamant Janie is in a great position, but he was also adamant Stelios's financial affairs are the reason why. It's no secret Marc has always been financially driven. It's due to his hard work and dedication that Suave is such a roaring success, but surely he wouldn't risk Janie having a broken heart for his own personal gain. Would he?

Smiling at a passing couple as they pose for photographs in front of the ocean, I try to make sense of what I have discovered on this trip. I came to Mykonos worrying Janie was using Stelios for his money, but I'm preparing to leave with the concern she's merely a pawn in his game. I always knew it would take someone special to couple up with Janie. She was never going to fall in love in the local coffee shop, or with the delivery guy who smiles at her ever so sweetly. A character as big and as bold as Janie deserves a story much bigger than that and a peculiar Greek billionaire with a sketchy past is amazingly, exactly what she was holding out for.

'Do you think Stelios loves Janie?' I say to Lianna, who quickly frowns back at me.

'Are you serious?' She replies, picking up a shell from the sand. 'Of course, he loves her!'

'How can you be so sure?' Pointing to another shell by her foot, I wait while she pops it into her pocket.

Li brushes her fringe out of her face and carries on walking. 'You just have to look at how much money Stelios has spent on her to answer that question...'

'Apart from the money side of things.' I groan, becoming tired of talking about Stelios's cash. 'Remove the extravagant gifts from the equation and what evidence have you seen that proves Stelios genuinely cares for Janie?'

Pursing her lips as she considers my question, Li looks down at the ground for a few seconds before shrugging her shoulders. 'I can't think of anything off the top of my head, but you are kind of putting me on the spot here...'

Sighing heavily, I turn my back to the wind and try to shake the feeling of nausea that is causing my skin to prickle. 'I've got a bad feeling about this, Li.'

'Why?' She asks, linking her arm through mine. 'Janie is a big girl. If this relationship turns out to be an extended holiday romance, so be it! Just let her enjoy it while it lasts.'

Realising she's the second person to say those words to me in as many days, I try and fail to believe them.

'That's the thing, Li. The wedge between Oliver and Janie is bigger than ever. If this goes on for much longer, I don't know if they'll be able to repair their relationship.' Sadness washes over me as I think back to how hard Oliver has worked at building bridges with his mother over the past few years. 'If this is nothing more than a fling, Janie and Oliver's relationship will have been destroyed for nothing.'

'I'm going to stay here.' Gina says confidently, before Lianna can reply.

'You don't fancy looking around the shops?' Turning to face her, I squint as the sun shines into my eyes. 'We're nearly there now.'

'No, you don't understand. I'm staying *here*, in Mykonos.' Gina says with a silly smile. 'I want to feel sand beneath my feet and sun on my skin every day of the year. I want to live by the ocean and wake up to a new adventure every single morning. I'm not going back...'

'I'm afraid holidays don't work like that, Gina.' Tugging on her arm, I throw my arms around her shoulders as a giant wave washes away our footprints. 'Not unless your name is *Janie*...'

Chapter 15

Slowly lifting my head off the pillow, I untangle myself from Oliver's arms and stretch out my legs. Despite being curled up in a luxurious bed all night, I barely slept a wink. As Oliver snored next to me, I stared up at the ceiling and tried my hardest to work out the enigmatic Stelios Christopoulos. I have scrutinised every aspect of his life for almost eight hours, yet I've come up with a big fat nothing.

He's a seventy-year-old billionaire with a reputation for being a womaniser and making bad decisions. With three failed marriages to his name, he's never had a lasting relationship and has a larger-than-life personality that makes Willy Wonka appear low-key. He keeps any signs of his character locked away in his bedroom, almost as though he's ashamed of who he really is. He believes throwing money at his problems will make them go away and apart from his business associates, his staff and his mother, I haven't seen him with a single friend.

Rubbing my tired eyes, I yawn as I walk across the room and push open the balcony doors. There are so many contradictions whooshing around my mind that I can't think straight. When we first met Stelios back at Suave, I didn't put much thought into who he really was. As far as I was concerned, he was the owner of a company we wished to work with and nothing more. Now, he is either Oliver's potential father-in-law or the man who caused the demise of his relationship with his mother. Right now, I'm not sure which is worse…

'Clara!' Hearing my name being called, I pop my head back into the room and spot Lianna hovering by the door. 'Clara, you've got to see this!'

'What is it?' I whisper, not wanting to wake Oliver.

'Just get out here!' Stamping her feet excitedly, she motions for me to hurry up.

Tugging down the hem of my nightshirt, I allow Li to drag me down the lobby and into the main building. Desperately trying to ensure my bum isn't showing, my jaw drops open as we come to a stop in the foyer, or at least, what *was* the foyer. The once minimalistic area has been completely transformed into a winter wonderland. Giant icicle-inspired baubles dangle from the ceiling, the walls have been delicately draped in flowing sheets of glitter and the palatial couches are nowhere to be seen. A dazzling display of silver roses creates an incredible archway for arriving guests, shielding them from the blue skies and sunshine outside.

'When did this happen?' Reaching out, I touch the soft petals of a rose and smile in awe when it sparkles back at me.

'Stelios had his team work right through the night.' Lianna explains. 'Isn't it amazing?'

Admiring the dramatic decorations, I nod in response and follow her through the hallway. Stelios's legendary parties are renowned in the fashion industry, but nothing could have prepared me for this. The villa is unrecognisable. Outside, Mykonos remains the same, but in here, it couldn't be more different.

'How many people are coming to the party?' I ask Lianna, who is busily snapping photos of a huge ice sculpture.

'I don't know, but I overheard Aris saying he was catering for a couple of hundred. Plus, some *huge* names are going to be here, apparently!'

'Like who?' I reply, following her outside, where Marc and Gina are enjoying a breakfast fit for a king. 'Giulia Romano?'

'*Shh!*' Letting out a shocked laugh, Li puts her fingers to her lips.

Flashing her a wink, I join Marc and Gina by the pool and pull out a chair at their table.

'What's going on out here?' I ask, frowning as I realise Marc is scribbling on a notepad. 'You're not working, are you? You promised to leave the business at home!'

Not bothering to look up, Marc continues to make messy scrawls on the pad.

'Do you have any idea who's going to be here tonight?' He stammers, frantically turning the page.

'Li was just telling me there are going to be some big celebrities attending.' Squinting at the paper, I try to get a glimpse of what he's writing. 'Anyone in particular you want to meet?'

'Celebrities?' Marc scoffs, taking off his glasses and rubbing the bridge of his nose. 'I couldn't care less about celebrities. I'm talking about businessmen, entrepreneurs, tycoons...'

Rolling my eyes, I zone out as Marc rambles about what an amazing opportunity this is to make connections within the industry. His refusal to stop working is incredibly frustrating. We have won with Suave. Our wish was granted. We have money and a successful company. We have everything we ever wanted. Why is he still pushing for more?

'When will it ever be enough for you?' I say under my breath, not realising before it's too late that I'm speaking out loud.

'What are you talking about?' Pausing with his pen to the paper, Marc finally looks up.

'I'm talking about this.' I reply, pointing to his pile of paperwork. 'You have Suave. Why do you want more?'

'Do you think *Stelios* just stopped at one business?' Marc says with a grin. 'Suave is just the beginning. If we continue to invest the profits, one day, we could have all of this, too.'

Pointing at the villa, he passes me the papers and I give them a fleeting glance.

'With the right connections and investments, just imagine what our life could be like. Clara, we could have it all...'

'That's the difference between you and me. I'm perfectly happy with my life as it is.' I say breezily, failing to see the lure of taking on yet more work. 'Our dream was Suave and our dream came true.'

Not wanting to get dragged into the disagreement, Gina and Lianna grab a couple of croissants from the breakfast tray and disappear into the building.

'Suave was our *original* dream.' Marc corrects, tapping his pen on the table. 'But our future could be even better. Our future could be *bigger* than Suave. I've been speaking to Stelios and he's been giving me all these tips. If we follow his lead, we could be just as happy as he is...'

'Happy?' I interject, unable to resist the laugh that tumbles out of my mouth. 'You really think all of this makes Stelios happy?'

'Of course, he's bloody happy! The guy is a *billionaire!*' Looking at me like I've lost my mind, Marc shakes his head. 'How could he not be happy?'

Realising nothing I say is going to change his mind, I simply nod back at him and push myself up.

'You do what you need to do, Marc, but Suave is enough for me.' I say sadly, handing him back the notepad. 'Just remember that you can't buy happiness. All that glitters is not gold...'

*   *   *

Catching a glimpse of myself in the mirror, I stop in the centre of the bustling room and admire my reflection. Earlier, Janie's prized hair and makeup team spent a good two hours preening me to perfection and the results are astonishing, to say the least. Gone are the tired bags under my eyes, gone are the frown lines that had set up home on my forehead and gone are the frizzy curls that framed them. In their place is a glowing complexion and skin that appears completely flawless. My once wild hair has been tamed into a beautiful chignon at the nape of my neck, finishing the polished look perfectly.

Smoothing down my lace cocktail dress, I clutch my glass and weave through the buzzing crowd. The Ice Party has been in full swing for around an hour now and things are starting to heat up. Hordes of paparazzi are gathered outside, the red carpet is flooded with posing partygoers and clusters of superstars are trying to remain inconspicuous as they sip their Champagne.

A few blotto businessmen laugh loudly in the dining room and I give them a cursory glance. Noticing Marc is with them, I shake my head and slip into the lively sea of people. Marc is one of the most stubborn people I know. I can tell him once or I can tell him a thousand times, but the outcome will still be the same. Once he has made his mind up about something, absolutely nothing will convince him otherwise.

Ignoring the heaviness in my chest, I force a smile and continue to work my way through the mob. A DJ is playing house music from a slick deck in the entrance hall, providing the perfect soundtrack to the exclusive party. After everything I had heard about Stelios's parties, I must admit to being slightly underwhelmed. Yes, the decorations are breathtaking, the music is amazing, the Champagne is flowing freely and some of the most famous people in the world are in attendance, but it all feels so hollow. It feels so false and void of all sentiment. All the ingredients needed to create the ultimate party are in place, but something is missing.

Waving at Aris as he whizzes past with a tray of drinks, I step into the dining room and stop when I spot Oliver and Stelios on the terrace. Both facing out to sea, they use their hands animatedly as they talk to one another. I can only see their backs, but something tells me there is an amicable air around them. They are finally communicating and that is a million steps in the right direction. Deciding not to disturb them, I scour the dining room for any signs of Janie.

With Stelios being predisposed with Oliver, she has to be around here somewhere. Squeezing through the mass of gyrating people, I accept a fresh flute of fizz from a passing waitress. The room is pulsing with people, making it almost impossible to spot my friends in the middle of the dance floor.

Raising my hand, I sway my shoulders in time to the music as they clock me through the crowd.

'Clara!' Lianna yells above the pulsing music. '*Clara!*'

Judging by the tipsy smiles on their faces, I'm guessing they're already a good few drinks ahead of me.

'Where have you been?' Gina asks, dancing around the ice sculpture with an enthusiastic party guest. 'You've been gone for ages!'

'I was just having a look around.' Positioning my back against the wall as to not get dragged into her energetic dance routine, I move aside as Vernon stops for a sip of his drink.

'It's amazing, ain't it?' He says excitedly, twisting his dreadlocks into a ponytail. 'Have you seen Bey and Jay?'

'Yes!' I lie, leaning to the left to check that Oliver is still with Stelios. 'Life made!'

Obviously deciding he's had the break he needed, Vernon takes Lianna by the hand and leads her to the centre of the dance floor before spinning her around. Snapping a photograph of them on my phone, I smile as another reveller joins me by the wall.

'They're certainly going for it!' He chuckles, pointing at Gina as she and her new-found partner dance up a storm.

'I know!' I laugh along as Gina teaches her friend the Macarena and clap my hands in time to the music.

Quickly picking it up, he copies her moves and holds out his arms in front of him. Resisting the urge to join in, I look over at my neighbouring guest as he inhales sharply and points to Gina's outstretched arm.

'What is it?' I ask, following his gaze to Gina's new tattoo.

Not responding with anything more than an embarrassed giggle, he laughs into the sleeve of his shirt before composing himself

'Do you speak Greek?' His voice is barely audible over the loud music, but I immediately know I'm not going to like what he has to say next.

Shaking my head in response, I turn my back to Gina.

'So, you don't know what that says?' My new friend laughs once more and I start to feel a little annoyed.

'She thinks it says *no regrets.*' I reply slowly, smiling as Lianna catches my eye. 'Why, what *does* it say?'

Cupping his hand around his mouth, he whispers into my ear and I hold on to the wall to steady himself.

'It says *what?*' I squeal, unable to hide my horror.

Clearing his throat, he looks over his shoulder to ensure no one is listening. 'I said, it says...'

'I heard you the first time!' I hiss, not quite believing what I've just heard. 'I was giving you a chance to tell me you were joking!'

'Totally *not* joking!' Chuckling to himself, he steals another glance at Gina's wrist as she twerks to a crowd of cheering people. 'Believe me, there's nothing funny about *that.*'

'Then why are you laughing?' I fire back, taking a much-needed gulp from my glass. 'This is awful!'

Nodding back at me, my new friend finishes his drink and grabs another from the pop-up bar behind us.

'Don't panic.' He says reassuringly. 'There's a laser removal place on the island. I actually have their card, if you want me to...'

Shooing him away, I watch him disappear into the crowd as my pulse races. I knew those dreaded tattoos were a bad idea. I bloody knew it! Suddenly remembering that both Lianna and Janie have the same foul-mouthed inking, I laugh in despair and hold my head in my hands.

'What is it?' Lianna asks, dragging Vernon my way and reaching for my glass. 'You look like you've seen a ghost. What did that guy say to you?'

My eyes flit down to Lianna's tattoo and I debate telling her the truth about her cherished new inking.

'Spit it out!' She presses, resting her hand on her hip. 'We're missing vital dancing time!'

The bass from the music thuds in my ears as Lianna stares at me expectantly.

Sometimes in life, you are presented with two choices and more often than not, ignorance is the best one.

'Nothing.' I reply with a grin, taking Lianna's hand and pulling her back onto the dance floor. 'Nothing at all...'

Chapter 16

Wiping mascara rings from under my eyes, I accept a spritz of perfume from the bathroom attendant and slip back into the party. The balls of my feet are aching from dancing, but the vast amount of fizz that's rolling around in my stomach is making me believe I can take on the world regardless. I haven't seen Oliver since I left him on the balcony with Stelios earlier, but that was hours ago and I'm becoming slightly concerned they might have thrown each other overboard.

Pausing to check I have fastened my handbag, I catch a glimpse of Janie in a grand room on the other side of the corridor. Slowly making my way across the lobby, I knock firmly on the open door and wait for a reply. Not getting an answer, I push my way inside and walk over to where she is sitting.

'Hey!' I say joyfully, placing a hand on her back as I come to a stop behind her. 'Why are you hiding in here?'

Swaying my hips in time to the music, I dance around the ornate dressing table and stop abruptly when I discover she's crying.

'Janie!' I exclaim. 'What is it? What's wrong?'

Dabbing at her cheeks with a scarlet handkerchief, Janie turns to face the mirror and sniffs loudly.

'I'm sorry, Clara.' She begins, her voice breaking. 'I was actually just coming to find you...'

My stomach drops as I slowly take a seat opposite her, preparing myself for what she is going to say next.

Her usually overly contoured face is wrought with pain, showing a hint of the woman she's so desperate to hide behind a mask of Botox and fillers. A pool of tears has created a damp patch on the hem of her blouse, indicating that she's been crying for quite some time.

'What is it?' I whisper. 'Janie, you're scaring me.'

Looking at her own reflection expressionlessly, she takes a deep breath before speaking.

'Before you guys came out here, I made a deal with Stelios.' Janie begins quietly, trying desperately hard to keep her voice steady. 'The deal was, if Oliver couldn't accept him, we would pull the plug on our relationship.'

Looking down at my lap, I feel my heart become physically heavier with each word that she says.

'It's never been about the Ice Party. The Ice Party was just a ruse to get you here.' She admits. 'Everything was riding on this vacation, Clara. *Everything*. That's why Stelios has gone above and beyond at every opportunity, making himself look like a crazy person. He's tried everything he can think of to get Oliver's approval. Even after I told him about our talk regarding the gifts, he still persisted with it in the hope that maybe, just maybe, he could make it work.' Pausing for breath, Janie looks down at the tattoo on her ankle. 'The poor guy's been a bag of nerves all week. He won't eat, he hasn't slept. He's tried everything to win Oliver over, but it just isn't going to happen.'

Staring back at her, I'm hit with an all-encompassing sense of guilt for questioning Stelios's wacky behaviour. It all makes sense now. Stelios wasn't playing some kind of underhand game with us.

His actions have been those of a desperate man. A man who is frantically trying to hold on to his relationship. This was him going all in. He placed all his chips on the final roll of the dice and I've judged him for it without giving him the chance to reveal the motivation behind it. I feel... well, I feel bloody awful.

'Stelios and I agreed if we didn't have Oliver's blessing by the end of these five days, I would fly home with you and we would draw a line beneath the last twelve months...'

'No!' I cry, shaking my head. 'You and Stelios are great together.'

Janie laughs and hangs her head sadly as yet another tear slips down her cheek.

'Every night, Stelios tells me how lucky he feels to have me in his life. He's a poker player, so he doesn't let many people see his emotional side, but once he lets you in, you discover he is the most wonderful man. These last twelve months have made me happier than I have ever been in my life. It has taken me many, *many* years to feel this way, but I don't want it at the expense of my relationship with my son.'

'You wouldn't ever lose Oliver...' I protest, as the music changes track.

'I'm already losing him!' Wiping her cheeks, Janie sobs into the handkerchief. 'I can feel him slipping further and further away from me and I won't stand for it! I've lost everything I've ever cared about, but I will be damned if I lose him, too.'

Sadness overcomes me as I look at my mother-in-law and try to break the awful spell that has fallen over us.

'I don't know what to say.' I mumble, not being able to look her in the eye. 'I really don't.'

'Then don't say anything.' Janie replies dejectedly, her voice lower than I have ever heard it before. 'There's nothing anyone can do now. Just go. Go and enjoy what is left of the party.'

'Janie...'

'Just go, Clara...'

Reluctantly standing up, I walk across the room and pause when I reach the door. Giving her a final look over my shoulder, I wait to see if she turns around before stepping back into the party.

I can feel the music pulsating through my body as I weave through the blanket of dancers and make my way to the balcony, where I left Oliver and Stelios earlier.

Dodging an inflatable flamingo, I carefully walk around the deserted pool. Various objects bob along the surface of the water, along with what appears to be a very sparkly dress and matching bra. Choosing to ignore the discarded clothing, I wander across the now-empty balcony and sigh in frustration.

The party is still in full swing, but due to the slight drop in temperature most of the guests have gravitated indoors. Taking a moment to enjoy the quiet, I lean over the balustrade and look up at the many stars that are illuminating the black sky. Janie's words buzz around my mind as I allow my eyes to close. Mykonos is such a beautiful island, but within the walls of this building there is so much sadness. I didn't see it before, but now it is impossible to ignore. The walls reek of desperation and the smiles seem to be hiding a whole world of fakery.

What first looked like a fairy tale ending for Janie has become a terribly sad rom-com. She hasn't been living a life of luxury out here, she's been worrying about it coming crashing down around her. She's simply been taking it one day at a time, searching for a way to keep both of the men in her life happy and failing miserably.

'What are you doing out here all alone?' A familiar voice asks.

Turning around, I smile as I see Oliver waving from the other side of the pool. With a beer in his hand and a grin on his face, he looks like the rest of the partygoers that are milling around the villa, but little does he know his mother is breaking her heart just a few feet away.

'What's with the long face?' He asks, obviously seeing past my fake smile as he comes to a stop beside me.

'It's...'

Before I can reply, a couple of drunk guests spill out onto the balcony and dive into the pool.

'It's... it's Gina's tattoo.' I lie, shrugging my shoulders and looking away.

'Oh...' Giving the rowdy swimmers a bewildered frown, he raises his eyebrows as they start to sing along to the music. 'What about the tattoo?'

Ushering me into a quieter corner of the balcony, Oliver points to a secluded bench.

'Well, it doesn't quite say what she thought it said, put it that way.' I whisper, taking a seat and turning my back to the breeze. 'You don't want to know the rest.'

'You can't leave me hanging like that! What does it say?' His eyes crinkle into a smile as he raises his beer bottle to his lips. 'It can't be that bad.'

Pulling him towards me, I whisper into his ear and lean back to see his reaction.

'You're kidding, right?' He stammers, his eyes widening with shock. 'That's hilarious! How? How do you know that?'

'A very appalled party guest took great pleasure in telling me so.' I reveal, watching the swimmers take turns in bombing into the water. 'I haven't told Gina. I'm of the firm opinion that what they don't know can't hurt them...'

'Wait a minute!' Oliver raises his hand to silence me and places his beer by his feet. 'Didn't my mom get the same tattoo?'

'And Li.' Having a flashback to the tattoo studio, I shake my head and giggle. 'All three of them. Stupid is as stupid does.'

'You mean... you mean... my *mom* has a tattoo that says...'

'Yes, she does and there's nothing anyone can do about it.' Nodding in response, I take the mention of Janie as the opportunity to bring up the elephant in the room.

'So, I saw you talking to Stelios before.' I begin, tucking a stray curl behind my ear. 'You seemed to be having a pretty deep conversation.'

'We were.' He confirms, peeling the label off his bottle and screwing it up.

'That's great!' Feeling a wave of hope wash over me, I sit up straight and smile. 'Tell me! What were you talking about?'

'Cars.' He says matter-of-factly. 'Lamborghinis, to be precise.'

A little stumped at his response, I wait for him to elaborate and frown when he doesn't.

While I was hoping for them to be having a momentous conversation about the meaning of life, the pair of them were speaking about nothing more than damn *cars*. They have four wheels and a horn. What else is there to possibly talk about?

'Did you manage to find some common ground with him?' I ask hopefully, crossing my fingers while I await his response.

'If you mean, do we both like fast cars, then yes.' Keeping his eyes fixed on mine, he smiles back at me.

'That's fantastic!' I exclaim, clasping my hands together with joy. 'I'm so happy to hear that.'

Reaching for his beer bottle, Oliver taps it against his leg and stares at the ocean. His brow furrows as he sits in complete silence, seemingly oblivious to the chaos in the swimming pool.

'Clara, I'm sorry to disappoint you, but Stelios and I aren't going to be buddies anytime soon.' He says quietly, all bravado absent from his voice. 'I've tried to get along with the guy, tonight especially, but I can't buy into it. I can't see past the *money-man* personality. I just don't believe who he claims to be. I'm sorry, but I don't.'

I hang my head in despair as I listen to Oliver's words, all the while knowing how much this is going to devastate Janie.

'Whatever my mom does and whoever she does it with is her decision, but I won't be a part of it...' He continues. 'I know how much you wanted this to work out, but when I believe someone is making a mistake, I'm not going to stick around and watch it happen.'

Completely lost for ways of trying to make Oliver see sense, I finally resign myself to the fact his mind is made up.

'I'm going to bed.' I mumble, no longer in the mood to party.

'Already?' Looking down at his watch, Oliver frowns as I push myself up. 'The night is still young!'

'The party is over, Oliver.' Locking eyes with him, I make no effort to hide how upset I am.
'It's time to call it a night.'

With a final frown, I turn on my heel and head back inside, taking my heavy heart with me...

Chapter 17

Tossing a black bikini into the suitcase, I blow a strand of hair out of my face and look around the room. Without my belongings scattered around the place, the spacious suite looks larger than ever, but bizarrely, it suddenly feels claustrophobic. The more I look at the empty magnolia walls, the more they appear to be closing in on me. For reasons I can't quite explain, I can't wait to get home to our apartment. To Noah, to Pumpkin and to my normal life. Who would've thought I would want to run away from a multi-million-pound mansion on an idyllic Greek island? The blue skies and abundant sunshine just aren't enough to keep me here. Mykonos might have stolen my heart, but Stelios's life here leaves me cold, empty and with a longing for normality.

'You're packing already?' Oliver asks, walking into the room with a steaming cup of coffee.

'I am. We have to leave for the airport at nine o'clock tonight, so I might as well get the packing out of the way now.' Bending down to retrieve a pair of Oliver's shorts from under the bed, I toss them into the case. 'What's left of yours to pack?'

'Can we at least have breakfast before we start all this?' Heading over to the wardrobe, Oliver pulls a pair of chinos off a hanger and hands them to me. 'I might not condone my mom's choice of partner, but I sure as hell love his breakfasts.'

Not being ready to joke about Stelios just yet, I smile thinly and nod as he disappears out of the room in search of food.

I haven't seen Janie since I left her last night and I'm not sure I want to. Half of me is hoping her threats to leave Stelios today were merely the result of her emotions running high and one too many glasses of wine, but something about the way she looked at me tells me otherwise.

Perching on the edge of the bed, I rub my temples and turn to face the sun, enjoying the sensation of warmth on my skin. I haven't breathed a word about Janie's ultimatum and I don't intend to, just in case she has a miraculous change of heart. The idea of someone walking away from the man they love to keep another person happy is heartbreaking, but without Oliver, Janie really doesn't have anyone.

Hearing footsteps enter the room once more, I look up to see Marc standing in the doorway.

'Hi...' He says quietly, shoving his hands into his shorts as he comes to a stop at the foot of the bed. 'Packing already?'

'What is it with men and leaving things to the last minute?' I grumble, pulling open random drawers to check for anything I've missed.

'You vanished from the party early last night.' Gingerly sitting down, Marc hands me a bottle of sunscreen from the bedside table. 'Oliver said you went to bed?'

'I just needed to be alone for a little while.' I reply, flipping the lid on the suitcase and shoving it across the bed to make some room. 'Besides, you seemed pretty preoccupied with the tycoon brigade.'

'That's actually what I came in here to talk to you about.' Marc says solemnly, rubbing his hands together as he always does when he's nervous. 'Dimitri Alafouzos, one of Stelios's closest allies, made me an offer to work with him...'

Rolling my eyes, I turn my back to Marc as he speaks and scour the bed sheets for discarded clothing. He knows my feelings towards his greedy attitude to business and yet he's persisted with it regardless.

'I don't want to hear it, Marc.' I grumble, attempting to push myself up. 'I really don't...'

'I turned him down.'

'You did what?' I reply, thinking I've misheard him.

'I turned them down.' Marc repeats seriously, a smile playing on his lips. 'You were right. I was chasing a dream I already had. *Suave* is what I always wanted and Suave is what I have.'

A little stunned by his revelation, I beam back at him proudly.

'My head was turned by the money and the lavish lifestyle that was on offer, but the truth is, I already have everything I could ever want. I own a share in the business that means so much to me, I have my best friends around me every day and I have more money than I ever dreamed of. Well, until Gina gets her hands on it.' Letting out a laugh, Marc reaches over and tilts my chin up. 'Are you... *crying?*'

'No!' I lie, quickly batting away my tears.

'Yes, you are!' Leaning across the bed, Marc ruffles my hair in an attempt to make me laugh. 'I knew you would be happy, but I didn't expect this...'

Not wanting to admit that my tears have more to do with Janie and less to do with his decision to walk away from more business deals, I shrug my shoulders and just go with it.

'Like I said, I'm proud of you.' Sniffing loudly, I wipe my cheeks on my arm and try to compose myself. 'Really proud.'

Marc nods back at me and we share a look that fills the silence perfectly.

'Anyway, that's enough of the deep chat.' He says happily, as laughter drifts into the room from outside. 'We have eleven hours before we leave for the airport. Let's go and enjoy them.'

Smiling in response, I wipe my face once more and allow him to drag me out of the suite. As we walk along the lobby more boisterous noise catches our attention, only this time, the shrieks of glee are accompanied by numerous splashing sounds.

'Where's that coming from?' Marc asks, stopping and trying to pinpoint the noise.

A series of squeals erupt behind us and I motion towards the indoor pool. The noise becomes louder and louder with each step that we take, until we push open the door and walk inside. Just as when we first arrived in Mykonos, Janie is floating around the immense pool with what appears to be a cocktail in her hand. The others are splashing around her, laughing joyfully as they bat one another with a variety of floating devices.

Too busy giggling at Lianna and Vernon as they wrestle for a beach ball, it takes me a moment to realise that Stelios is also in there and most unbelievably of all, so is Oliver.

'I thought you guys were having breakfast!' I exclaim, sitting on the side of the pool and dangling my legs into the cool water.

'Eating is cheating!' Lianna cheers, adjusting her bikini and clambering onto an inflatable cupcake with the ball under her arm. 'We can eat back home.'

'Still, I wouldn't say no to a bacon sandwich.' Feeling my stomach growl, I debate leaving them to it and giving in to the lure of fried food.

'Swim first, bacon later!' Vernon replies, swimming to the edge of the pool. 'When are we next gonna be able to do *this* before breakfast?'

'Hopefully, not too long.' Stelios answers on my behalf. 'You, my family, are welcome here any time at all. You just say and I book the flights.'

My gaze automatically moves to Janie, who is hiding behind a giant pair of sunglasses.

'You're so kind, Stelios!' Lianna gushes, kicking her legs to stay afloat. 'We would love to come again. Wouldn't we, guys?'

The others chime in agreement and I bite my lip anxiously. As far as I'm aware, the others don't have a clue about Janie's ultimatum and I'm still clueless as to whether she's going to go through with it. As though reading my mind, Janie claps her hands together to get everyone's attention.

'Alright, while I've got all you gremlins together, I want to thank you for coming out here to visit us.' Janie says appreciatively. 'It's been so good to see all of you, because regardless of what you might think, I *have* missed you. I've missed you very much. Some more than others…'

'We've missed you, too!' I reply, from my position by the side of the pool.

'Yeah, it's not the same without you scouring Owen's drawers for Rémy Martin.' Marc teases, swimming over to Janie's inflatable flamingo. 'All that cognac is really building up in the office, but don't worry, it'll be waiting for you when you come back.'

Joining in with the others as they laugh along with Marc, I can't help thinking that the Rémy Martin might not have to wait for much longer.

'Before we put all this soppy business behind us, there's just one last thing I wanted to ask you.' Pausing to remove her sunglasses, Janie looks at me briefly before speaking. 'You're all aware that you were invited here to attend the Ice Party, but I must confess to having an ulterior motive...'

My ears ring as the others fall into silence. This is it. This is the moment it all boils down to. Janie's future in Mykonos hangs on the outcome of this conversation.

'I think you'll all agree that before you flew out here, Stelios was a business associate and nothing more. These past five days have given you a chance to get to know the man behind the name.' Reaching for Stelios's hand under the surface of the water, Janie takes a deep breath before continuing. 'So, do Mr Christopoulos and I get your blessing?'

Not hesitating for a second, Marc, Gina, Li and Vernon immediately speak up.

'Of course!'

'Absolutely!'

'We love Stelios!'

'The guy is a legend!'

Listening to them throw a whole dictionary of compliments at Stelios, a sudden rage bubbles in the pit of my stomach. Their opinions of Stelios are based on nothing more than the money he has thrown at them. They have no idea how desperate Stelios is and how hard he has tried to prove himself to them. They haven't devoted a mere five minutes to learning about Stelios and his life.

Despite my efforts to stop it, the fury shoots up my windpipe and explodes in my mouth like hot lava.

'How can you say that?' I blurt out, unable to stop the words from tumbling out. 'None of you have taken the time to get to know Stelios.'

Looking at the shocked faces that are staring back at me I know I have opened a can of worms, but once I start I just can't stop.

'I bet you don't know a single thing more about Stelios than you did before we arrived.' I continue, not caring in the slightest that I may be speaking out of turn. 'All you have done is sweep up his gifts and over-the-top gestures, which little do you know he gave out of sheer desperation.'

Adrenaline whooshes through my body as I switch my focus to Stelios.

'The gifts aren't needed, Stelios. You don't need to *buy* people's affection. If they like you, they like you. Your finances shouldn't come into it. The people who like you purely for what you can offer them don't really like you at all. Their love and their loyalty are false. Just like the rest of this place...'

Stelios blinks repeatedly and steadies himself on Janie's shoulder, looking as though the wind has been well and truly knocked out of him.

'On paper, you have the perfect life.' I persist. 'You have more money than most people could spend in a lifetime, yet you can't enjoy it. You confine your personality and your real character to a single room, afraid of what your business contacts would think if they saw who you really are.'

A wave of sadness hits Stelios's eyes and I know I have hit a nerve, but something inside me refuses to stop.

'Why do you care what they think? You've made it. You made it a long time ago. You don't need to vie for their approval. You don't need their business. In fact, you don't need *any* of this.' Motioning around the pool, I point to Ioannis and Georgios, who are standing in the corner and doing their best to pretend this conversation isn't happening. 'You don't need a hundred members of staff. You don't the security guards, the fleets of limousines and to be woken by maids bearing breakfasts. You have the most incredible kitchen I have ever seen. Enjoy it! Cook in it, dine in it and discover what your wealth has truly brought you. I bet you don't even know where your cutlery is kept, do you?'

Stelios hangs his head in shame and sighs deeply. 'No. No, I do not.'

'Then why have it?' I ask, aware that I'm testing his limits. 'Why have any of it if you can't enjoy it?'

There's a long pause where you could hear a pin drop, before Stelios finally speaks up.

'I don't know. I don't know why I have it.' He stammers, like I've asked him the most difficult question imaginable. 'I just keep working. Keep working means I keep buying. The money doesn't mean anything to me anymore. That's why I give it away. Like I give to you. What is mine, is yours. I don't care. I don't care about money, but people care about me when I give them the money. You see?'

'But you don't need to do that, Stelios. That is what I am trying to explain.' I say gently. 'You're a good man, we would have liked you without the gifts. Right, guys?'

Looking at the others, I'm pleased to see them all agreeing.

'You're a great person, Stelios. A fascinating person, in fact.' Marc starts, holding his hands out in front of him. 'I just didn't bother to find that out and for that, I'm sorry. I think we all are. We allowed ourselves to get carried away with your lifestyle. I'm sure you can understand how easy it is to get sucked up into your frankly mind-blowing world.'

Embarrassed murmurs come from the rest of the gang as I look on, proud that my friends can admit when they've been wrong.

'We didn't mean to take advantage of your good nature.' Lianna mumbles guiltily. 'You have been so kind to us and I guess we just got lost in the moment, but I do think you're a fabulous man and most definitely the right one for Janie.'

'Me too.' Gina adds. 'With or without the money.'

'Yeah, me too.' Reaching out, Vernon shakes Stelios's hand firmly.

The look of relief on Janie's face causes the mood to instantly lift, but I am very aware there's still one person yet to speak.

'Oliver?' Janie asks timidly, holding on to Stelios to stop herself from bobbing around in the water. 'Do we get your blessing?'

The atmosphere suddenly becomes unbearably tense as Oliver runs a hand through his hair in silence. Seven pairs of eyes burn into him, waiting for him to make the next move.

'I'm sorry, Mom, but he just isn't right for you.' He says confidently, fixing his stare on Janie. 'I've tried to see the draw here, but I keep coming up with a blank. Apart from the ability to throw bags of money at his problems and hope they go away, what does he offer you?'

Janie attempts to speak, but Oliver doesn't wait for her to respond.

'I appreciate that you have given us your hospitality, Stelios, I really do. For that, I can't fault you, but as far as being the man for my mom, I don't think so. You're so caught up in your cash and your materialistic lifestyle that you don't have a clue how the world works. You're so detached from reality and so sheltered from real life. You're... you're a fake.'

Feeling my jaw fall open, I slowly turn around to look at Stelios and brace myself for his comeback.

'Fake?' Stelios repeats, as if he has never heard the word before in his entire life. 'You think I am fake and... what are the other things you say?'

'Detached, sheltered and don't have a clue how the world works.' Gina offers, rather unhelpfully.

Nodding slowly, Stelios smooths down his moustache. The vibe in the room, which was temporarily lifted by the positive response from the others, is now lower than ever. Not daring to look at Janie, the sadness inside me grows as I glance at Oliver. I can't make him accept Stelios. No one can. He's his own person and as such, he is entitled to his own opinion, but that doesn't alter how immensely disappointed I feel inside.

'You give me two hours.' Stelios says intently, locking eyes with Oliver and holding up two fingers. 'Two hours and if after that, you *still* think I am fake and detached and clueless, then I walk away. I walk away from my Janie.'

An inflatable pizza floats aimlessly around the pool as we all turn to look at Oliver. Gently nudging him under the surface of the water, I smile encouragingly and hope he gives Stelios the dignity of one last shot.

'Fine.' He grumbles, a scowl taking over his tanned face. 'Two hours...'

Not hesitating, Stelios lets go of Janie's float and shouts in Greek to Ioannis and Georgios, who swiftly jump into action and grab a handful of towels from the dressing room. Without saying a word, Stelios swims to the edge of the pool and pulls himself up the steps.

'Please...' Standing on the poolside dripping in water, he holds out a towel to a bemused Oliver before leading the way outside.

Watching the two of them disappear out of the room, leaving a trail of soggy footprints behind them, I scramble to my feet and run to the window with the others.

'What's going on?' Lianna asks, leaning against me in her wet bikini. 'They're not going to get in the limo soaking wet, are they?'

Peering out of the glass, I look on as Ioannis ushers them into the vehicle and gives Calix the signal to drive.

'Where do you think they're going?' I say to Janie, who is standing behind us with glassy eyes as the limo purrs away from the building. 'Any guesses?'

Seemingly frozen to the spot, Janie blinks a few times before inhaling deeply and smiling.

'I have a pretty good idea...'

Chapter 18

Carefully making my way along the shabby stone steps, I hold on to the wall to steady myself and wince as a sharp shard pricks my hand. The old paintwork has peeled due to many years of being subjected to the sun's glare, making it feel rough beneath my palm as I follow Janie down the ancient stairway. I can almost see the heat rising from the cobbled path, which is shielded on both sides by old white buildings. Just like the last five days, the sun has burnt through any clouds that dared to cross its path and as a result, we are being treated to a sheet of pure blue sky.

Resting my hands on my hips as we arrive at the bottom, I walk a few metres to the right and discover that we're in an old fishing harbour. An array of quaint shops and quirky cafes line the pavement, each one offering traditional souvenirs, locally made wine and cute keepsakes. Colourful canopies provide shade for the many locals and tourists, who are enjoying themselves in the morning sun. Elderly men are happily playing cards, a smattering of women leisurely browse the stalls and groups of families are chatting over lunch.

'Are you *sure* this is the place?' Gina asks, wiping a bead of sweat from her brow. 'Why would Stelios bring Oliver here?'

Stopping to say hello to a friendly stallholder, Janie points to the crumbling buildings up on the hill behind us.

'This is where Stelios grew up.' She explains. 'He lived right there, in that apartment. The second window to the left.'

Stepping back, I squint through my sunglasses and look up at the white apartment block we have just walked past. The tired structure has seen better days and the overgrown bushes around it make the tattered exterior appear even more neglected.

'Are you sure?' Vernon replies sceptically, frowning as he studies the building closely. 'I thought Stelios was born into his riches?'

'You gotta be kidding me.' Shaking her head, Janie slowly makes her way along the harbour. 'Stelios had it rough as a boy. His father was always off with other women and Konni tried her hardest to make ends meet, but it wasn't easy. Far from it. At just twelve years old, Stelios would go fishing in this very port. Along with a neighbour, he would take a whole bunch of bait and not return until he had enough for dinner. He barely had an education, never mind a full stomach. Stelios and his brother didn't know what money was until their twenties when they went into business together. It's been a long hard road for both of them. Rags to riches just doesn't cover it.'

Stopping outside a picturesque bakery, I feel a lump form in my throat. Stelios isn't a delusional billionaire with no idea of the meaning of life. He's a boy from a disadvantaged family who miraculously managed to claw his way to the top. He shouldn't be judged for his incredible success, he should be praised for it.

'I had no idea.' I mumble in complete shock. 'I really didn't.'

'Me neither.' Kicking off her sandals, Gina quickly puts them back on again when she realises the floor is too hot to walk on. 'I presumed he was born with a silver spoon in his mouth.'

'Well, you were wrong to presume.' Janie replies, heading for a strip of golden sand by the water. 'If you would have taken the time to ask Stelios about his upbringing, he would have been happy to tell you. Happy to tell you and happy that you were interested enough to ask...'

Gina's cheeks flush as we fall into an embarrassed silence. Janie's right. Instead of getting to know Stelios and welcoming him into our circle, all four of them greedily accepted his gifts without caring about the motive behind them. And I am no better. I might not have revelled in his generosity, but I judged him all the same.

Absorbing the humiliation that I quite rightly deserve, I stop to look at a tiny souvenir stall as the others walk on. Various trinkets and ornaments twinkle back at me and I study them carefully. From creative fridge magnets to bracelets as blue as the ocean, there's something here for everyone, well, everyone except Noah. His request for a unicorn comes rushing back to me and I give the rack one last glance before continuing on my way.

'Can I help you?' A cheery voice asks behind me.

Looking back, I spot an elderly lady stepping out from behind the counter.

'I was just looking for a gift for my son.' I explain, taking a few steps back towards the stall. 'He's asked for a *unicorn*.'

'A unicorn?' Twirling around the rack of souvenirs, the helpful lady holds up her hand and disappears behind a sheer curtain.

Keeping one eye on the others to ensure I don't get left behind, I smile as the stallholder returns with a tiny bottle.

'I don't have any unicorns, but I do have this...' She says eagerly, holding out the glass bottle.

'What is it?' Turning it over in my hands, I marvel at the multicoloured grains.

'It's *Unicorn Dust*. You make a wish and throw a pinch over your shoulder. Dreams do come true, if only we wish hard enough.' Leaning in closer, she whispers into my ear. 'But between you and me, it's coloured sand from right here in Mykonos.'

Grinning happily, I reach into my bag for my purse. 'We could all use a little Unicorn Dust from time to time. I'll take it.'

Quickly stuffing the cash into her pouch, the stallholder passes me some change and shakes my hand. 'Thank you. Enjoy Mykonos!'

Smiling back at her, I tip a few grains of the bright sand into my palm and throw them over my shoulder before rushing after the others.

With the harbour becoming increasingly busy, it takes me good a few minutes to locate the others by the edge of the water. While the rest of the gang take photos in front of the idyllic backdrop, I follow Janie's lead in taking a seat on the sand. Sunshine sparkles on the surface of the ocean, almost sending me into a hypnotic state as I allow my eyes to relax and watch the many fishing boats bobbing around in the bay.

This quaint fishing village is a world away from Stelios's luxury mansion, but it's a million times more beautiful. The true essence of Mykonos is all around us and unlike the palatial villa, it is actually being enjoyed for what it is. There's no pretentious food, there are no flash cars or rich men in suits talking about making yet more money. It simply does what it says on the tin and for that, I absolutely adore it.

'While we are waiting, I have something I would like to say.' Gina suddenly declares, as the others tire of their photo shoot and collapse onto the ground. 'And I don't want any of you, especially you, Marc, to say anything before I finish.'

Shuffling around so that I can see Gina's face without being blinded by the sun, I cross my legs and get comfortable.

'I have decided... to stay in Mykonos and before you all laugh or tell me I have end-of-holiday blues, I have put a *lot* of thought into this.' Smacking her lips together, Gina paces up and down by the water's edge. 'Travel is good for the soul, we all know that, but this trip has reminded me just how much I love it. I've had a strange feeling in the pit of my stomach for a long time now, longer than I can care to remember, but I've never quite been able to determine the cause of it. However, just five days on this beautiful island have made it crystal clear. It was *wanderlust*. Wanderlust is what has been making me feel so... unsettled. I need to spread my wings one final time. I need to believe this isn't the end for me...'

'One final time? The end?' Marc repeats, almost angrily. 'What the hell are you talking about? Are you sick? Do you need to lie down?'

'No, I am not sick, Marc.' Laughing lightly, Gina offers him a hand to help him to his feet. 'I knew you would react like this, but that's okay, because I've had a chance to process things and you haven't. With a little time, you will come to the same conclusion I have.'

Gaping at Gina, I try to work out if she's joking. You would think that I've known her long enough to know when she's kidding, but something about her expression is throwing me off. She looks delirious, high on life and dare I say it, a little manic.

'Have you had a bump on the head?' Widening his eyes, Marc looks at Gina like she has lost her mind. 'Because if you have, we need to get you checked out.'

'No! I have simply come to the realisation that this is what I want.' She exclaims, keeping her crazed smile firmly in place. 'It would be incredible for us as a family. Just think about it. This could be like Australia all over again. We could have a new adventure. The kids could wake up to this every single day. They could learn another culture and experience a different way of life that would enrich their souls.'

Suddenly realising she might actually be serious, I glance over at Lianna and give her a nudge.

'Gina, we own a fantastic apartment in one of the best cities in the world. We have no money worries and a fabulous business.' Marc takes a step towards her and stuffs his hands into his pockets. 'Our life is amazing just as it is.'

'I know all that.' Bending down, Gina grabs a handful of sand and lets it fall through her fingers like confetti. 'But is that really enough for you?'

'What the... yes, of course, it is enough for me!' Marc cries, sounding completely flabbergasted. 'Gina, you're starting to freak me out. Where is this coming from?'

Looking out over the water, Gina shrugs her shoulders. Her dark hair billows in the breeze as we all watch her silhouette against the stunning backdrop.

'I'm scared, Marc.' She whispers, in a voice so quiet I can barely hear her. 'I'm absolutely petrified.'

'Petrified about what?' Despite the vast amount of colour he has gained this week, Marc's face pales to a deathly shade of white. 'What is it? Tell me!'

'I'm going to... I'm going to be...' Gina's voice trails off into a series of sobs as Marc wraps his arms around her protectively.

'Going to be what?' He asks desperately. 'Whatever it is, we can work through it together. It's going to be okay.'

Bawling loudly, Gina wipes her face and turns her back to the wind.

'I'm going to be... *forty*.' She wails, spitting the word *forty* out like it's poisonous.

I knew it! I bloody knew it! I told anyone who would listen that Gina was on the verge of a midlife crisis, but no one believed me. No one took me seriously and yet here we are, witnessing Gina announce her plans to throw down her anchor in Mykonos and become a Greek gypsy.

'You can't be serious?' Holding her at arm's length, a slight smile plays on Marc's lips. 'Is that really what this is about? You're afraid of being forty?'

Howling like a baby, Gina nods and wipes her wet cheeks.

'Gina! You really had me going there!' Marc laughs and visibly breathes a sigh of relief. 'Why didn't you say you were having a midlife crisis?'

Hearing the *M-word*, Gina's tears come to an abrupt stop. 'Because I am *not* having a midlife crisis.'

'Are you kidding me? You just told me you were doing a Shirley Valentine and staying in Mykonos!' Marc lets out a laugh and despite her best efforts to stop it, Gina joins in. 'Forty isn't a big deal. Age is just a number...'

'That's easy for you to say.' Gina replies haughtily. 'You're years away from the dreaded forty.'

'Forty is the new thirty!' Marc protests. 'Your forties are going to be the best years of your life. We are in a better position now than we ever have been. The last ten years have been great, but the next ten are going to truly amazing. You don't want to run away from it, believe me. You want to embrace it, because there is so much more to look forward to than what we leave behind.'

Holding her head in her hands, Gina, rests her chin on Marc's chest. 'I just don't want you to think I'm past it.'

'Past it?' Marc repeats, cupping her face in his hands. 'Gina, you keep me on my toes every single day of the week. Each morning I wake up excited about what you will do to make me smile next. You might be a few years ahead of me in the numbers game, but inside, you might as well be twenty-one.'

'Really?' Gina looks at Marc as though that's the most romantic thing she's ever heard. 'Do you really mean that?'

'Of course, I mean it!' He confirms, causing Gina to break into a smile. 'So, does that mean we can stay in London?'

Nodding enthusiastically, Gina reaches up and kisses Marc on the lips as the rest of us whoop and cheer at their happy reunion.

'Oh, I do love a happy ending!' Lianna trills, pulling Marc and Gina down onto the sand next to her. 'You guys are adorable.'

The words *happy* and *ending* cause my stomach to flip as I'm reminded why we're here. They say that every story has a happy ending if you stop in the right place, but life isn't a fairy tale and happily ever after isn't guaranteed for anyone. All we can do is hope, pray and keep believing that everything happens for a reason...

Chapter 19

Glancing at my watch, I drop down the straps on my camisole and yawn into the back of my hand. We have been sitting in the fishing port for at least an hour, but there's still no sign of them. Despite the fact that time is running out for Stelios and his two-hour ultimatum, the mood in the group is surprisingly chipper. Well, it's chipper for everyone but Janie. Staring straight ahead as the rest of the gang sunbathes around her, she looks totally and completely lost.

'Janie, where exactly do you think Oliver and Stelios are?' I ask, shuffling closer to her.

Picking up a smooth pebble, Janie holds it to her chest and shrugs. 'To be honest, I don't really know. They could be here, they could be somewhere I've never even thought of, but if I know Stelios like I think I know Stelios, he will be here, eventually.'

Nodding along, I cross my legs and study her face closely. 'You didn't mean what you said last night, did you? Because we all say things when we're upset. It doesn't mean we believe them. You should hear the things I say to Oliver when I'm upset...'

Dropping the pebble into the sand, Janie shakes her head. 'I wish I could say that I didn't, but I meant every word.'

Replying with a sad smile, I make an attempt at steering the conversation to a different topic. Janie has made her decision. There's no point in dwelling on it now. What will be, will be.

'So, we leave for the airport in a matter of hours. It could be your final chance to tell me what your tattoo from Stelios means.'

Twisting her leg to reveal the inking, Janie runs her fingers over the tattoo fondly. 'Let's just say it was an offer.'

'An offer?' I reply, frowning at the tattoo. 'An offer of what?'

'A proposition.' Clearly choosing her words carefully, Janie purses her lips. 'A suggestion, an intention, a... *proposal*.'

'A proposal?' The word hits me like a bullet as I stare at Janie dumfounded. 'A *proposal?* Does that mean...'

Before I can finish my sentence, Vernon jumps up and whistles loudly.

'There they are!' He yells, pointing over the water. '*Oliver! Over here!*'

Scrambling to my feet, I follow his finger and wave my arms around to get their attention. In a tiny fishing boat, which has seen many, *many* better days, Stelios and Oliver are using a pair of tatty oars to manoeuvre the boat back to shore. They're pretty far away, but I can see quite clearly that Oliver has a toasty forehead from being in the sun without sunscreen. Where the hell have they been? There's nothing but water as far as the eye can see. Unless they've been sitting in the middle of the ocean, I fail to see what they could possibly have been doing.

Waiting until they are merely a few metres away from us, Oliver and Stelios jump out of the boat and push it up onto the sand. Not daring to breathe a word, I try to assess their faces for a clue as to how this impromptu *fishing trip* went. Both of them appear completely deadpan as they come to a stop in front of us, neither giving anything away.

'Well?' Janie asks, clasping her hands together in front of her. 'How did it go?'

The air is thick with tension as Stelios slowly holds out his hand and waits to see if Oliver takes it. Silently willing him on, I bite my lip as Oliver looks down at Stelios's outstretched hand. His brow is furrowed into a frown, causing Stelios's stern expression to waver. Just as I am losing hope and mentally booking Janie a seat on the plane home, Oliver takes Stelios's hand in his and shakes it firmly.

'It turns out he's not that bad after all.' Oliver says with a grin, clapping Stelios on the back. 'I'm not ready to call him dad just yet, but he'll do, for now...'

Running across the sand, Janie envelopes Oliver in a huge bear hug. Not wanting to ruin this moment for them, I step to the side and give Stelios the thumbs-up.

'What did you say to him?' I whisper, stumbling backwards as he embraces me warmly. 'How did you make him change his mind?'

'I simply showed him the real me.' Blinking back tears as he motions around the harbour, Stelios sighs heavily. '*This* is the real me. This is who I am. Stelios Agapetos Christopoulos, is made of all of this.'

Smiling at the emotion in his voice, I beam brightly as Janie and Oliver re-join us.

'You were, right, Clara. I do not need the people and the many vehicles or the big house. Well, maybe the big house, but things have become... out of control.' Using his hands to emphasise his point, Stelios continues with his speech. 'I remember a time where all I desired was food in my stomach. I was so happy when I first paid my bills and still had money in my pocket. Very happy. I haven't been that happy since. All the things I thought I needed, I do not, and this is what I have realised.'

Finally stopping for breath, Stelios takes my hands in his and squeezes them tightly.
'Thank you, Clara. You have opened my eyes to where I have been going wrong for so long.'

Feeling my cheeks flush, I nod back at him as he walks over to where Ioannis and Georgios are keeping guard.

'Ioannis and Georgios, your work here is done.' Stelios says warmly, shaking both of their hands twice over. 'You can go.'

Raising their eyebrows, Ioannis and Georgios appear completely bewildered.

'Go?' Ioannis repeats, taking out his earpiece. 'You want us to go?'

'Yes. Please go and enjoy the day.' Stelios persists, reaching into his pocket and handing them wads of crisp notes that are slightly wet at the corners from the water. 'Spend time with your families, buy them a nice meal and just... *live*.'

Looking at the money in their hands, which would buy their families food for the next ten years, Ioannis and Georgios grin from ear to ear. After muttering a few words to Stelios in Greek, they shake his hand once again before heading off over the sand.

Watching them walk away, I look over at Oliver and feel my stomach flip when I see him grinning happily.

'I am sorry I tried to purchase your approval of me.' Stelios says seriously, addressing the entire group. 'I am, from the bottom of my heart, sorry, but my heart is pure. My heart is good.'

'It is better than good.' Janie says, happy tears spilling down her cheeks. 'Pure as gold.'

There's an emotional silence, where the only sound comes from the waves kissing the shore, before Oliver finally breaks it.

'Alright, that's enough of the mushy stuff.' He says confidently, wrapping an arm around Janie's shoulders. 'We came here for a party and more importantly, we came here to make sure my mom was in safe hands. Both of which we have accomplished. Now, let's eat.'

Vernon and Marc start to clap and before long, the others join in. Cheering as loud as my lungs will allow, I jump up and down on the spot. People at the cafes behind us join in with the clapping, regardless of not knowing what it is we are celebrating.

Holding his hands in the air to silence us, Stelios begins to walk across the sand and signals for the rest of us to follow him.

'Come with me! I know just the place...'

*   *   *

Biting into the most delicious pitta bread I have ever tasted, I lick a dollop of tzatziki from my little finger and swoon. For the past twenty minutes we have been sitting on the pavement outside a food shack, devouring gyros and listening to stories about Stelios's upbringing. My cheeks are aching from laughing, but my greed for the gyro means I keep eating regardless.

'These gyros, my patéras... my father, we would fish all morning and sit right here eating gyros.' Wiping his moustache on a paper napkin, Stelios smiles adoringly at Janie as she rests her head on his shoulder. 'The best gyros on the island, with the best people.'

'Amen!' Gina cheers, between sips of ice-cold beer. 'I second that!'

Looking at the pile of sandals and flip-flops in front of us, I realise the bottom of my feet are black from walking barefoot, but it just makes me smile even more. This is exactly what I wanted from this holiday. Foreign voices are all around me, I have traditional Greek food in my stomach and the sun is shining beautifully onto the perfect blue water ahead. This is Greece at its finest and I wouldn't want to be anywhere else in the world.

Tuning back in to the conversation as Stelios continues to share tales from his childhood, I turn to Oliver and wipe a blob of tzatziki from his chin.

'So, what happened on the boat?' I whisper, draping my legs across his lap. 'I'm dying to know what went down out there.'

'The boat was unexpected, I'll tell you that much.' Shaking his head slowly, Oliver reaches for his beer and hugs me with his spare arm. 'When Calix pulled up here, I sure wasn't expecting to be taken out on the ocean like that. Half of me thought he was going to throw me overboard.'

I smile back at him, not wanting to speak in case I break his flow.

'Everything I believed about Stelios was wrong. The man I thought he was doesn't even come close to the truth.' He pauses and screws his napkin up into a small ball. 'Sure, he's flashy and a bit of an ass sometimes, but Stelios isn't a bad guy. Once he opened up to me about his upbringing, I could see the man my mom was so desperate for us to meet. To come from such hardship is mind-blowing.'

Quietly overjoyed by his admission, I nod along proudly.

'I hold up my hands and admit that on this occasion, I got it wrong and I have never been happier to be wrong in all my life. I hated the idea of my mom being out here and I allowed that to cloud my judgement.' He says softly, looking over at Janie and smiling. 'Now I can fly back, safe in the knowledge that my mom is going to be okay.'

Replying with nothing more than a happy smile, I return to my gyro as a cheer drifts out of a Greek restaurant to our left. The sound of glasses clinking together encourages me to pick up my own bottle of beer and I hold out in front of the others.

'Cheers, guys!' I sing, beaming brightly. 'To Stelios!'

'Please, I am not worthy.' Stelios places a hand on his heart, clearly touched by my gesture. 'To Mykonos!'

'To Mykonos!' We all shout in unison.

Taking a sip of the amber bubbles, I lean back and take in the smiles of my friends. Well, not my friends. Stelios was right about one thing. These guys aren't my friends, they *are* my family. We're one big, slightly dysfunctional, completely non-traditional family and I wouldn't have it any other way.

Tipping my head back, I enjoy the sensation of the ocean breeze on my face and inhale deeply. This might not have been the typical package holiday, but I am leaving with the holiday glow that everyone aims to achieve.

Slowly peeling open my eyes, I smile as Janie and Stelios share a loving glance while the rest of the gang chat amongst themselves. Their eyes soften as they beam at one another, completely oblivious to anything and everything around them. Finally breaking their stare, Janie points to her ankle tattoo and grins.

Suddenly remembering her revelation about the meaning behind the tattoo, I watch in awe as she waits for Stelios to respond. Not taking his eyes away from hers, Stelios nods eagerly as Janie leans over and kisses his cheek. Catching my eye, she winks and reaches for Stelios's hand. Did she just? Does that mean? A squeal from Janie all but confirms to me that it does.

Clasping my hands over my mouth, my heart pounds as I resist the urge to scream out loud. My mind flits back to the bet on a proposal and I giggle to myself. I've just won. Vernon and Gina were right, a proposal *was* on the cards. It just so happens that it has taken place in a way they never imagined. Deciding to keep this snippet of information to myself for now, I raise my bottle to my lips and smile back at Janie. Happiness pours out of her as she joins in with the conversation, all the while keeping her fingers entwined with Stelios's.

I might have won the bet, but Janie is the real winner here. Despite the many obstacles life has thrown her way, despite the many diversions and dead-ends she has hit on her journey, Janie has at long last found true love. With a little luck and maybe a sprinkle of Unicorn Dust, she has found her happily ever after.

Although, the older you get, you realise happily ever after isn't a fairy tale, it's a choice and it seems that Janie has *finally* made the right one...

To be continued...

The Clara Andrews Series

Follow Lacey London on Twitter

@thelaceylondon

Have you read the other books in the Clara series?

Meet Clara Andrews

The fantastic first book in the bestselling Clara series by Lacey London.

The Clara series takes us on a journey through the minefields of dating, wedding-day nerves, motherhood, Barbados, America, Mykonos and beyond.

It all starts with an unfortunate first meeting...

Being young, free and single, Clara Andrews thought she had it all.

A fabulous job in the fashion industry, a buzzing social life and the world's greatest best friends are all that her heart desires. But when a chance meeting introduces her to Oliver, a devastatingly handsome American designer, Clara has her head turned.

Trying to keep the focus on her work, Clara finds her heart stolen by lavish restaurants and luxury hotels.

As things get flirty, Clara reminds herself that office relationships are against the rules. So, when a sudden memory of an evening out leads her to a gorgeous barman, she decides to see where it goes.

Clara soon finds out that dating two men isn't as easy as it seems.

Will she be able to play the field without getting played herself?

Join Clara as she finds herself landing in and out of trouble, reaffirming friendships, discovering truths and uncovering secrets.

It's time to Meet Clara Andrews... your new best friend.

Clara Meets the Parents

Grab a margarita, slip on your sunglasses and join Clara on her fun-filled trip to Mexico.

Almost a year has passed since Clara Andrews found love in the arms of delectable American Oliver Morgan, and things are starting to heat up.

The nights of tequila shots and bodycon dresses are now a distant memory, but a content Clara couldn't be happier about it.

And it's not just Clara who things have changed for...

Marc is adjusting to his new role as Baby Daddy, and Lianna is lost in the arms of the hunky Dan once again.

With her friends busy with their own lives, Clara is ecstatic when Oliver declares it time to meet the Texan in-laws.

Discovering that the introduction will take place on the sandy beaches of Mexico simply adds to her excitement, but things aren't set to be smooth sailing...

Will Clara be able to win over Oliver's audacious mother?

What secrets will unfold when she finds an ally in the beautiful and captivating Erica?

Clara is going to need a little more than sun and sand to get through this one...

Meet Clara Morgan

"How do you tell your best friend that her wedding dress is utterly vile?"

Wedding bells are ringing for Clara and Oliver in Meet Clara Morgan - the much-anticipated instalment in the Clara Andrews series.

When Clara, Lianna and Gina all find themselves engaged at the same time, it soon becomes clear that things are going to get a little crazy.

With Clara's best friends planning their own impending nuptials, it's not long before Oliver enlists the help of Janie, his feisty Texan mother, to help Clara plan the wedding of her dreams.

However, it's not long before Clara discovers that Janie's vision of the perfect wedding day is more than a little different to her own.

Will Clara be able to cope with her shameless mother-in-law?

What will happen when a groom gets cold feet?

And how will Clara handle a blast from the past who makes a reappearance in the most unexpected way possible?

Join Clara and the gang as three very different

brides, plan three very different weddings.

With each one looking for the perfect fairy-tale ending, who will get their happily ever after?

Clara at Christmas

With snowflakes falling and fairy lights twinkling brightly, it can only mean one thing - Christmas shall very soon be upon us.

With just twenty-five days to go until the big day, Clara finds herself dealing with more than just the usual festive stresses.

Her plans to host the perfect Christmas Day for her American in-laws are ambushed by her BFF's clichéd meltdown at turning thirty.

With a best friend on the verge of a midlife crisis, putting Christmas dinner on the table isn't the only thing Clara has got to worry about this year.

Taking on the role of Best Friend/Therapist, Head Chef and Party Planner is much harder than Clara had anticipated.

With the clock ticking, can Clara pull things together - or will Christmas Day turn out to be the December disaster that she is so desperate to avoid?

Join Clara and the gang in this festive instalment and discover what life-changing gifts are waiting for them under the tree this year...

Meet Baby Morgan

The cot has been bought, the nursery has been decorated and a name has been chosen. All that is missing is the baby himself...

It's fair to say that pregnancy hasn't been the joyous journey that Clara had anticipated.

Extreme morning sickness, swollen ankles and crude cravings have plagued her for months, and now that she has gone over her due date, Clara is desperate to get this baby out of her.

With a lovely new home in the leafy, affluent village of Spring Oak, Clara and Oliver are ready to start this new chapter in their lives.

As Lianna is enjoying the success of her interior design firm, Periwinkle, Clara turns to the women of the village for company.

The once inseparable duo finds themselves at different points in their lives, and for the first time in Clara and Lianna's friendship, the cracks start to show.

Will motherhood turn out to be everything that Clara ever dreamed of?

Which naughty neighbour has a sizzling secret that she so desperately wants to keep hidden?

Laugh, smile and cry with Clara as she embarks on her journey to motherhood.

A journey that has some unexpected bumps along the way.

Bumps that she never expected...

Clara in the Caribbean

Pour yourself a rum punch and get ready to jet off to Barbados in this sun-soaked trip to the Caribbean.

Almost a year has floated by since Clara returned to the Big Smoke and she couldn't be happier to be back in her city.

With the perfect husband, her best friends for neighbours and a beautiful baby boy, Clara feels like every aspect of her life has finally fallen into place.

And it's not just Clara who things are going well for...

The Strokers have made the move back from the land Down Under and Lianna is on cloud nine.

Not only has Li been jetting across the globe with her interior design firm, Periwinkle, she has also met the man of her dreams... again.

For the past twelve months, Lianna has been having a long-distance relationship with Vernon Clarke - a handsome man she met a year earlier on the beautiful island of Barbados.

After spending just seven short days together, Lianna decided that Vernon was the man for her and they have been Skype smooching ever

since.

Due to Li's rather disastrous dating history, it's fair to say that Clara is more than a little dubious about Vernon being 'The One'.

So, when her neighbours invite Clara to their villa in the Caribbean, she can't resist the chance of checking out the mysterious Vernon for herself.

Has Lianna finally found true love?

Will Vernon turn out to a knight in shining armour or just another fool in tin foil?

Clara in America

The Sunshine State is calling!

All aboard this drama-filled trip to sunny Florida...

With Clara struggling to find the perfect present for her baby boy's second birthday, she is pleasantly surprised when her crazy mother-in-law, Janie, sends them tickets to Orlando.

After a horrendous flight, a mix-up at the airport and a let-down with the weather, Clara begins to question their decision to fly out to America.

Despite the initial setbacks, the excitement of Orlando gets a hold of them and the Morgans start to enjoy the fabulous Sunshine State.

Too busy having fun in the Florida sun, Clara tries to ignore the nagging feeling that something isn't quite right.

Does Janie's impromptu act of kindness have a hidden agenda?

Just as things start to look up, Janie drops a bombshell that none of them saw coming.

Can Clara stop Janie from making a huge mistake, or has Oliver's audacious mother finally gone too far?

Join Clara as she gets swept up in a world of fast food, sunshine and roller coasters.

With Janie refusing to play by the rules, it looks like the Morgans are in for a bumpy ride...

Clara in the Middle

"Common sense is a flower that doesn't grow in everyone's garden…"

It's been six months since Clara's crazy mother-in-law took up residence in the Morgan's spare bedroom and things are starting to get strained.

Between bringing booty calls back to the apartment and teaching Noah curse words, Janie's behaviour has become worse than ever.

When she agreed to this temporary arrangement, Clara knew it was only a matter of time before there would be fireworks. But with Oliver seemingly oblivious to Janie's outrageous actions, Clara feels like she has nowhere to turn.

Thankfully for Clara, she has a fluffy new puppy and a job at her friend's lavish florist to take her mind off the problems at home.

Clara finds herself feeling extremely grateful for her fabulous circle of friends, but when one of them puts her in an incredibly awkward situation, she starts to feel more alone than ever.

Will Janie's bad behaviour finally push a

wedge between Clara and Oliver?

How will Clara react when Eve asks her for the biggest favour you could ever ask?

With Clara feeling like she is stuck in the middle of so many sticky situations, will she be able to keep everybody happy?

Join Clara and the gang as they tackle more family dramas, laugh until they cry, and test their friendships to the absolute limit.

Clara's Last Christmas

"Even the strongest blizzards start with a single snowflake."

Just a few months ago, life seemed pretty rosy indeed...

With Lianna back in London for good, Clara had been enjoying every second with her best friend.

From blinged-up baby shopping with Eve to wedding planning with a delirious Dawn, Clara and her friends were happier than ever.

Unfortunately, they are brought back to reality when just weeks before Christmas, Oliver and Marc discover that their jobs are in jeopardy.

With Clara helping Eve to prepare for two new arrivals, news that Suave is going into administration rocks her to the core.

It may be December, but the prospect of being jobless at Christmas means that not everyone is feeling festive.

Should they give up on Suave and move on, or can the gang work as one to rescue the company that brought them all together?

Can Clara and her friends save Suave in time for Christmas?

Jump into Clara's world for a heart-warming, hilarious ride in Clara's Last Christmas!

Clara Bounces Back

"If there were no bumps in the road, life would be an awfully dull journey..."

After taking control of Suave just six months ago, Clara and the gang are walking on sunshine. However, it's not long before the reality of owning the business starts to hit home.

With the repercussions of the Giulia Romano sex tape still hitting the company hard, Owen starts to question the stability of his investment.

Not wanting to give up on their dream, Clara and her friends have one last shot at turning things around before they throw in the towel for good.

When Marc spots a way to use the sex tape to their advantage, the gang have no choice but to put their future in the hands of Clara's brazen mother-in-law.

With a chickenpox epidemic taking over the group, Janie's outrageous persona starts to cause friction amongst Clara's group of friends.

Can they trust Janie enough to act on behalf of the company, or will her audacious behaviour

be the final nail in the coffin for not only Suave, but their friendship with the Lakes?

Slip back into Clara's world and join the old gang as they reunite in this much-anticipated continuation of the series!

Clara's Greek Adventure

"Palm trees, ocean breeze, salty air and sun-kissed hair..."

Janie, an eccentric billionaire and Mykonos.

What could possibly go wrong?

Almost a year has drifted by since Suave secured the Ianthe contract and things are going very well indeed.

With the success of the partnership shooting Suave for the stars, the gang are closer than ever and living life to the max.

Enjoying their new-found wealth proves to be a fun and exciting time for Clara and her friends, but there's one thing that's keeping a smile from Oliver's face...

After declaring their love for one another twelve months ago, Janie and Stelios have been loving life in Stelios's luxury mansion in Mykonos, but not everyone is happy for them.

Oliver has made no secret of his detest for Stelios Christopoulos, and that hatred seems to be growing stronger by the day.

However, when the gang are invited to attend Stelios's exclusive Ice Party in Mykonos, Oliver has no choice but to put his own feelings aside and represent Suave.

Will this trip give Stelios a chance to finally win over Oliver?

Is Janie's love for Stelios based on more than just fast cars and money?

With five whole days under the Greek sun awaiting them, will they all leave as friends, or will the holiday be the final straw for Oliver and his mother?

Join Clara and her friends as they jet to Mykonos and discover what Janie's heart really holds.

Have you read the other books by Lacey London?

The Anxiety Girl Series

Anxiety Girl
Anxiety Girl Falls Again
Anxiety Girl Breaks Free

Anxiety Girl

Sadie Valentine is just like you and I, or so she was...

Set in the glitzy and glamorous Cheshire village of Alderley Edge, Anxiety Girl is a story surrounding the struggles of a beautiful young lady who thought she had it all.

Once a normal-ish woman, mental illness wasn't something that Sadie really thought about, but when the three evils, anxiety, panic and depression creep into her life, Sadie wonders if she will ever see the light again.

With her best friend, Aldo, by her side, can Sadie crawl out of the impossibly dark hole and take back control of her life?

Once you have hit rock bottom, there's only one way to go...

Lacey London has spoken publicly about her own struggles with anxiety and hopes that Sadie will help other sufferers realise that there is light at the end of the tunnel.

The characters in this novel might be fictitious, but the feelings and emotions experienced are very real.

Anxiety Girl Falls Again

After an emotional voyage through the minefield of anxiety and depression, Sadie decides to use her experience with mental health to help others.

Becoming a counsellor for the support group that once helped her takes Sadie's life in a completely new direction and she soon finds herself absorbed in her new role.

Knowing that she's aiding other sufferers through their darkest days gives her the ultimate job satisfaction, but when a mysterious and troubled man attends Anxiety Anonymous, Sadie wonders if she is out of her depth.

Dealing with Aidan Wilder proves trickier than Sadie expected and it's not long before those closest to her start to express their concerns.

What led a dishevelled Aidan to the support group?

As Sadie delves further into his life, her own demons make themselves known.

Will unearthing Aidan's story cause Sadie to fall back into the dark world she fought so hard to escape?

Anxiety Girl Breaks Free

Life is full of difficult questions, but **this** shouldn't be one of them...

Aidan is back. He is standing right here in front of me. This could be the start of something special. It **should** be the start of something special. Only life isn't always that simple, is it?

With Aidan back in Cheshire and work on Blossom View well under way, it would appear that things are finally falling into place for Sadie Valentine.

Her career with the charity is keeping her busy, Aldo is enjoying being off the market and her relationship with her mother is starting to heal, but it's not long before the cracks start to show.

Not wanting to succumb to the anxiety that is slowly casting a shadow over her newly-found happiness, Sadie attempts to press on with her life regardless.

As Sadie tries to paper over the cracks, blasts from the past return to tip her world upside down in ways she could never have imagined.

With her limits being tested once again, can Sadie use her experience and strength to break free from her anxiety once and for all?

They say that the past should stay buried, but what if some ghosts simply refuse to lie low?

The Mollie McQueen Series

Mollie McQueen is NOT Getting Divorced

Mollie McQueen is NOT Having a Baby

Mollie McQueen is NOT Having Botox

Mollie McQueen is NOT Ruining Christmas

Mollie McQueen is NOT Getting Divorced

"Whoever said money can't buy happiness, obviously never paid for a divorce..."

When Mollie McQueen turned thirty, she awoke with a determination to live her best life.

Her marriage to Max was the first thing to come under scrutiny and on one sexless night in May, Mollie decided that their relationship was over.

However, when a grouchy divorce lawyer convinces Mollie there's a chance she could bow out of this life being eaten alive by a pack of cats, she starts to search for an alternative.

Opening the can of worms that is her marriage makes Mollie realise she might not be as blameless as she initially thought...

Will Mollie be able to rescue her marriage or has the lure of a life without wet towels on the bed turned her head?

One thing is for sure... Mollie McQueen is NOT getting divorced.

Mollie McQueen is NOT Having a Baby

Some women want babies, others just want to sleep like one.

Since completing their marriage counselling with therapist to the stars, Evangelina Hamilton, life in the McQueen household was looking rather cosy indeed.

Max was flying high in his new career and Mollie was finally turning her attention to renovating the house that was falling down around them.

Forming an unlikely friendship with none other than the office pariah, Timothy Slease, results in Mollie making it her mission to help him find love.

With a house to renovate and Tim's love life to sprinkle Cupid dust over, the shock of a possible pregnancy hits Mollie harder than a Ronda Rousey left hook.

Not being the type of woman who goes weak at the knees at the sight of a dirty nappy, Mollie resorts to her old coping mechanism of burying her head in the sand.

Picturing her life with a child in tow makes Mollie question everything she was previously so sure of.

With Aunt Flo refusing to play ball, house renovation

catastrophes and dating disasters might not be the only things that Mollie McQueen is expecting...

Mollie McQueen is NOT Having Botox

"Maybe she was born with it, maybe it's Botox…"

It's November. Mollie's least favourite time of the year. The days are short and the nights are cold, but when her nearest and dearest get hit with a case of the midlife crisis bug, it gives her something more than the terrible weather to complain about.

Watching her parents and in-laws putting themselves through chemical peels and hair transplants causes Mollie to make it her mission to prove that the natural approach to anti-aging is best.

Spending time with her eccentric and outlandish neighbour, Mrs Heckles, just adds to Mollie's firm opinion that growing old gracefully is the only attitude to have.

Enlisting the help of Tim's ageless girlfriend, can Mollie convince her loved ones to step away from the scalpel and learn to love the person in the mirror?

With snails, urine and some rather unorthodox tools at her disposal, Mollie certainly has a hard task on her hands, but with a troublesome cat, a huge work opportunity and a friend heading for heartache, will they all be taught a lesson in the cruellest way possible?

One thing is for sure, Mollie McQueen is NOT Having Botox.

Mollie McQueen is NOT Ruining Christmas

"Be naughty and save Santa a trip. It's better for the planet…"

There was little over a week to go until Christmas Day, but Mollie McQueen hadn't sent a single card. She hadn't purchased one gift, and she hadn't decked the halls with anything other than mountains of wet laundry.

Usually, come the first of December, the McQueen house resembled Santa's grotto. Stockings would hang from the fireplace, his and hers advent calendars would be propped up on the mantlepiece, and the two sparkly polar bears bought by Mollie's mother would stand proudly on the windowsill.

This year, all was quiet on the Christmas front. The door was missing its usual wreath, the sprig of mistletoe was absent from the hallway, and the alcove in the living room was minus the retro tree that Mollie normally insisted on rolling out on the first day of December.

When Mollie first announced her plans to strip Christmas back to basics, she received nothing but negative feedback. Max accused her of trying to ruin Christmas, Margot advised her to chuck back a daily vitamin D pill in a bid to rediscover her Christmas spirit, and Mrs Heckles had taken to singing Christmas carols through Mollie's letterbox.

Despite their grumbling, Mollie was determined to prove to everyone that you could enjoy Christmas without falling victim to the endless marketing campaigns that emotionally blackmailed you into purchasing unnecessary gifts for people who would rather have a pack of socks and a slice of Yule log.

With her no-Christmas Christmas amassing quite the guestlist, Mollie had an almighty task on her hands.

Can she convince her nearest and dearest that the true meaning of Christmas had nothing to do with expensive gifts and garish decorations?

One thing's for sure, Mollie McQueen is NOT Ruining Christmas.

Printed in Poland
by Amazon Fulfillment
Poland Sp. z o.o., Wrocław

57762297R00148